# Guitar Class Method
## Volume 2

## Contents






*Visit us at www.melbay.com — E-mail us at email@melbay.com*

# READING TABLATURE

Tablature is simply a drawing of the 6 strings of the guitar with numbers showing you to-either pick a string open or in which fret to press a string down to produce the note called for in the music.

The tablature will appear throughout this book directly under each note of music showing which string and in which fret every note is found on the guitar.

Shown below are examples of tablature with an explanation of each item.

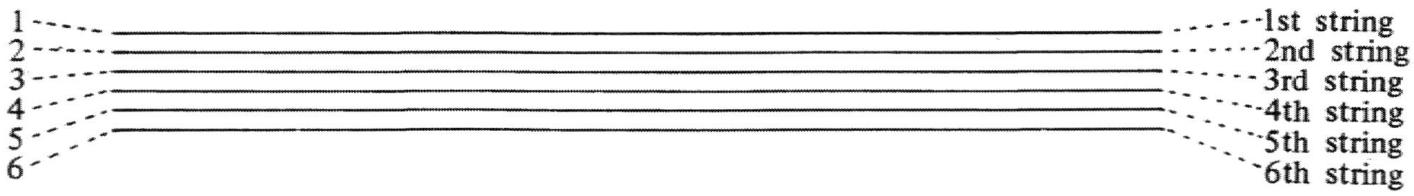


There are six lines in the tablature, one for each string on the guitar as shown above.

The numbers placed on the tablature lines show in which fret to press down the left hand fingers.

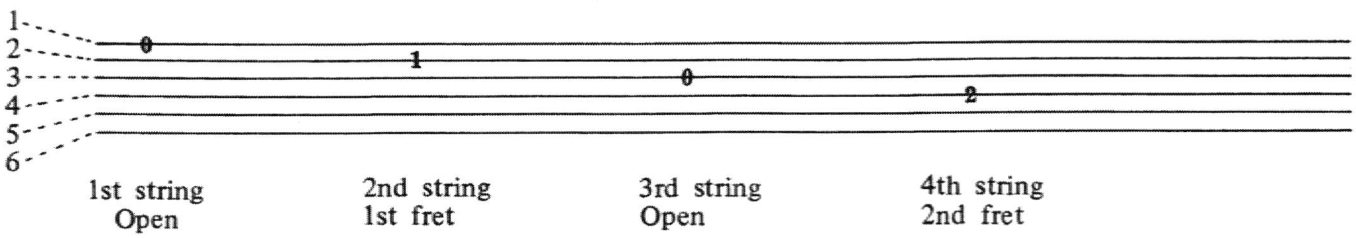


# COUNTING TIME IN TABLATURE

Counting time in tablature will be exactly the same as in regular musical notation, using a time signature at the beginning, with measures separated by bar lines, and with stems being used for the different time values.

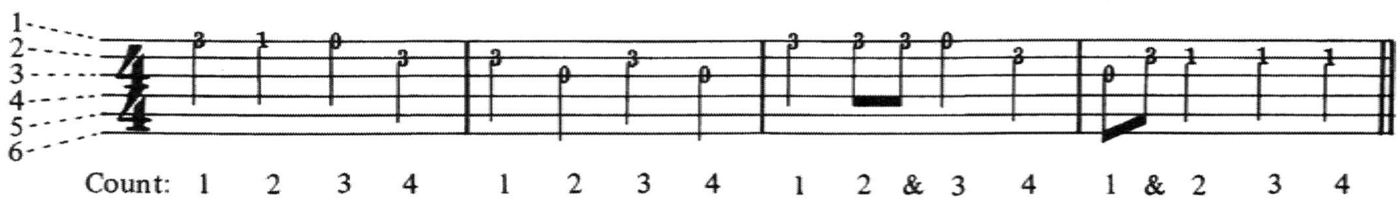


The only difference in tablature counting will be that if a note is to be held longer than one count, it will be shown as follows:

The first count will have the regular quarter note stem and will be connected to one additional quarter note stem for each additional count the note is to be held.

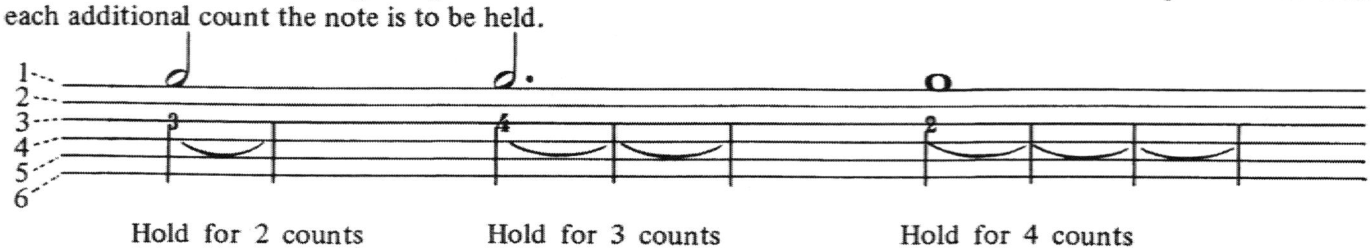


A dot (.) adds ½ Count to a tone:  = 1½ Count  = ½ Count

# CHORD STRUMMING SOLOS

# COUNTRY STYLE ACCOMPANIMENT

# BLUEGRASS STYLE SOLOS

# WILDWOOD FLOWER

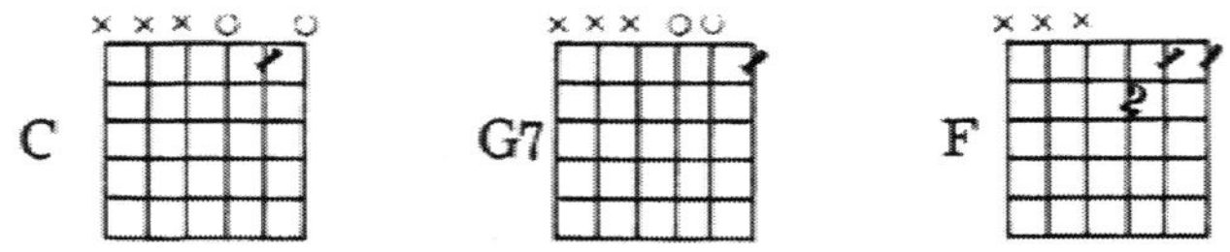


Bluegrass Song

# CIDER THROUGH A STRAW

# OH, HOW I LOVE JESUS

# HARD, AIN'T IT HARD

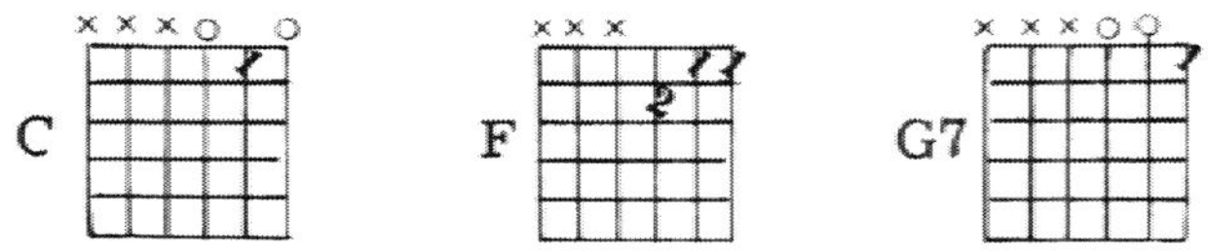

# MARINE HYMN

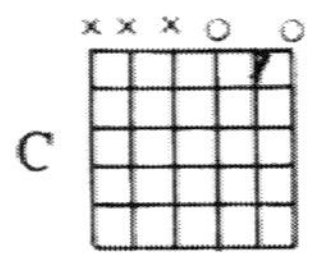

C


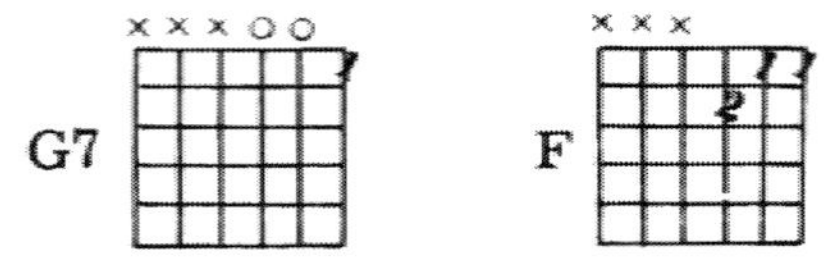

G7
F

March
From the halls of Mon - te - zu - ma To the
shores of Tri - po - li we will fight our
Coun - try's bat - tles in the air on land and
sea First to fight for right and free - dom and to
keep our hon - or clean We are proud to claim the
ti - tle of U - nit - ed States Ma - rines.

# MY OLD FRIEND

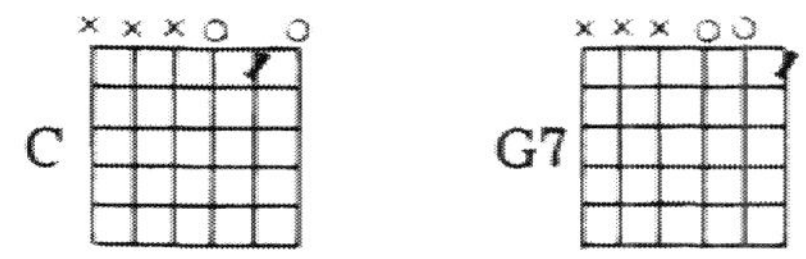


Traditional Melody
Words by Steve Griffin

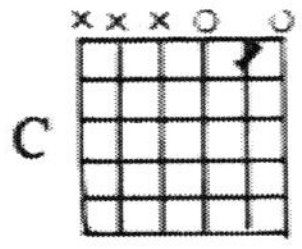


# SWEET HOUR OF PRAYER

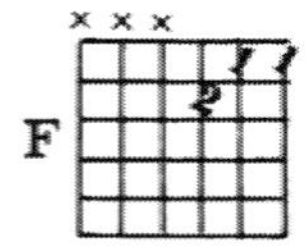


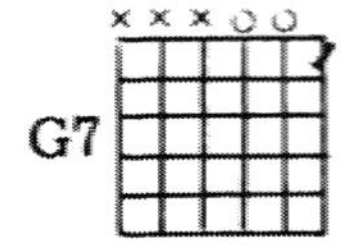


William W. Walford
William B. Bradbury

# GO TELL AUNT RHODY

# Old Time Religion

# Cindy

Folk Song

# COUNTRY STYLE ACCOMPANIMENT

On these "Country Style" arrangements, some may play the melody and some may play the accompaniment part. The accompaniment is the most important part, at this point, for learning purposes.

## Amazing Grace

# Frankie and Johnnie

**Easy tempo** **Folk Blues**

# Careless Love

American Folk Song

# Cowboy Jack

Traditional

# Crawdad Song

Traditional

# Look Down That Lonely Road

Spiritual

# This Train

Spiritual

# Cielito Lindo

Mexican Love Song

# BLUEGRASS STYLE SOLOS
## Cripple Creek

Arr. Tommy Flint

# Bile Them Cabbage Down

**Brightly**

**Arr. Tommy Flint**

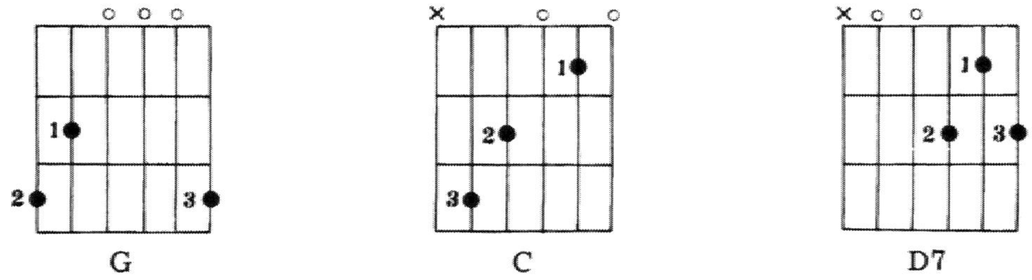

# Mr. Peale's Ram

Tommy Flint

# John Henry

Arr. Tommy Flint

# Butler County Breakdown

Tommy Flint

**Brightly**

G7
D7
G7
C
D7
F
G7
C
F
C

# Chippewa Hill

Tommy Flint

Medium

F
C
D7
G
C
G
D7
C
G
D7
G

# Old Joe Clark

Arr. Tommy Flint

**Moderately fast**

CAN BE PLAYED THIS WAY

Eighth notes may be used instead of the quarter notes.
Alternate picking should be used.
The chords will still be played as quarter notes.

**Example**

# Sally Goodun

Arr. Tommy Flint

* The first B note in measure number five is played on the third string at the fourth fret.

The line means to slide into the note. Place the finger one or two frets lower (second or third fret) and slide rapidly to the fourth fret on the count of one.

# The Laurel Mountains

Tommy Flint

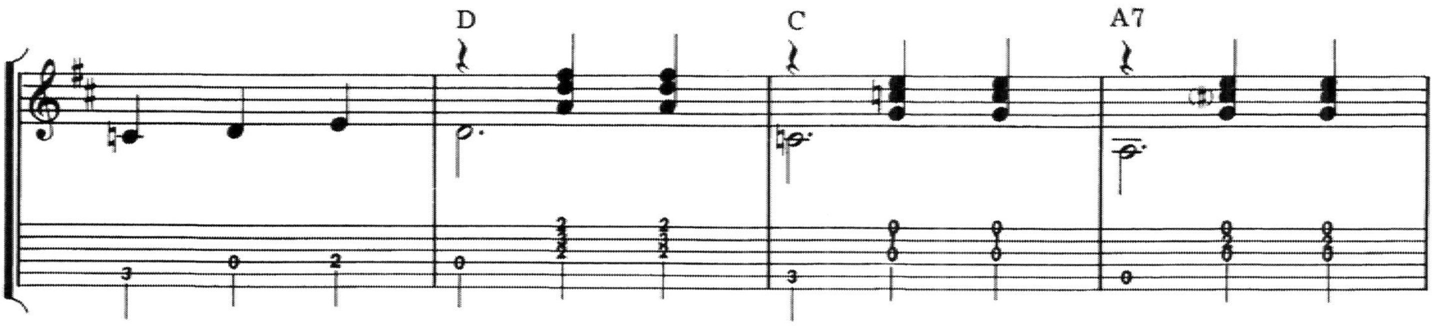

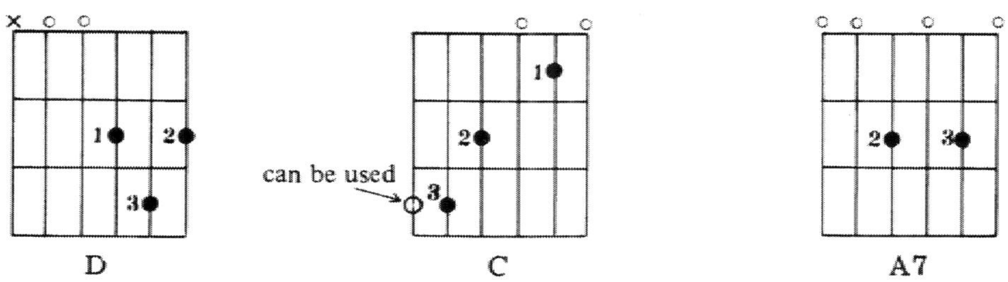


# Turkey Buzzard

**Tommy Flint**

**Fast**

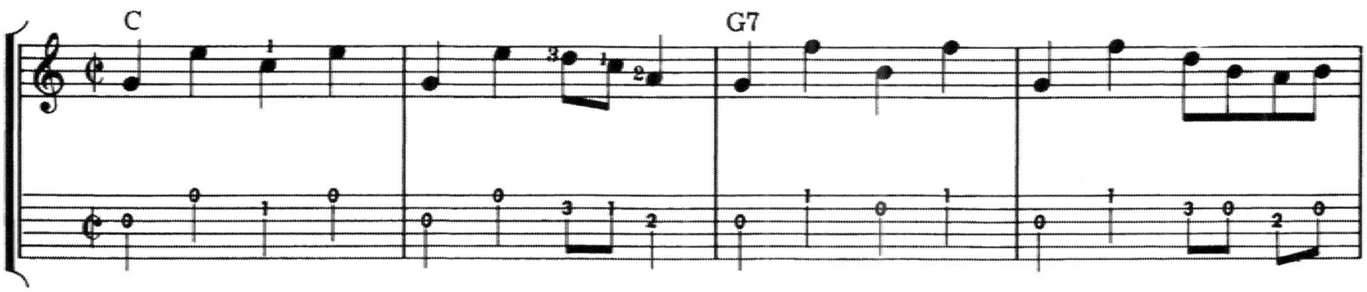


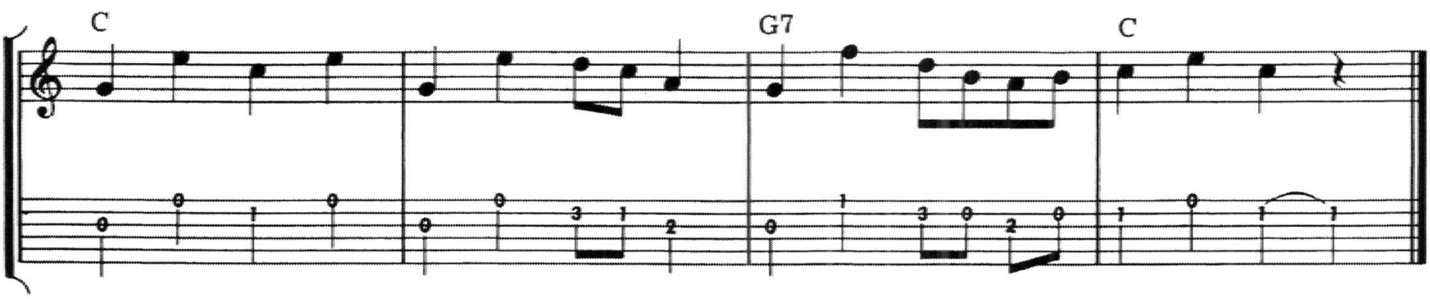

# BLUES AND CONTEMPORARY SOUNDS

# BACK DOOR BLUES

SUGGESTED STRUM : BLUES - ROCK

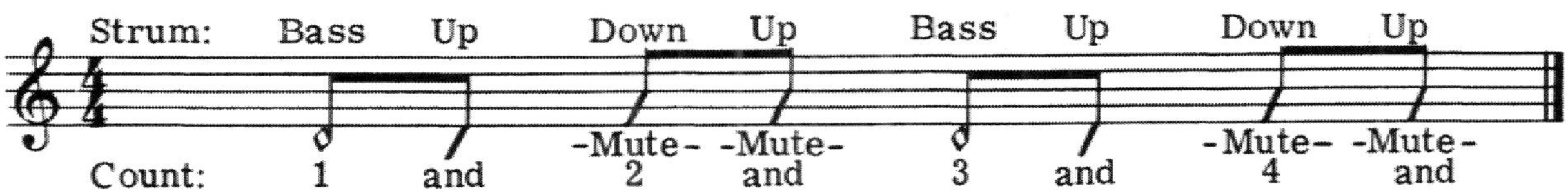


CHORDS USED :

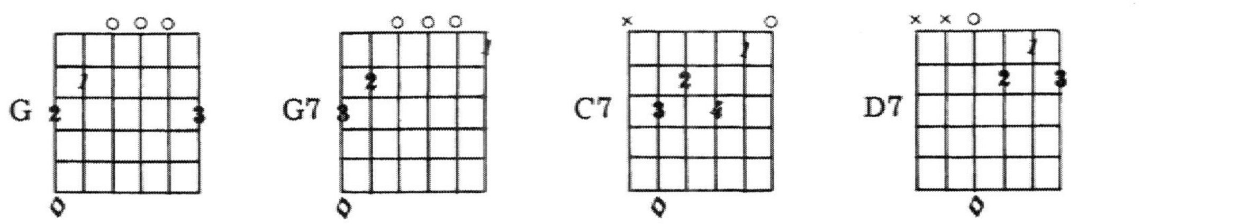


◊ = Indicates single bass note

# LEADING ME ON

SUGGESTED STRUM : EASY ROCK

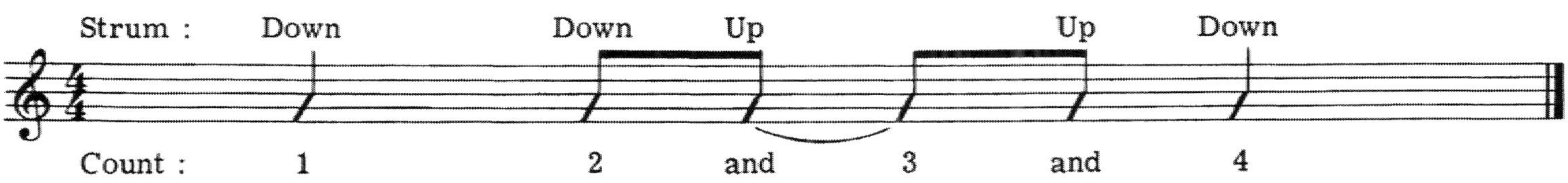


CHORDS USED:

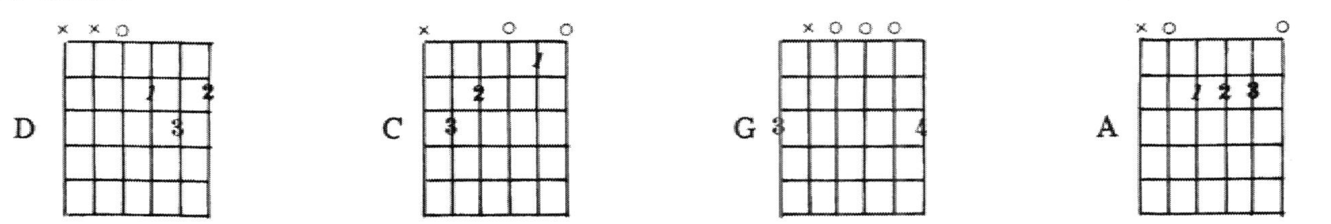

# FREEWAY

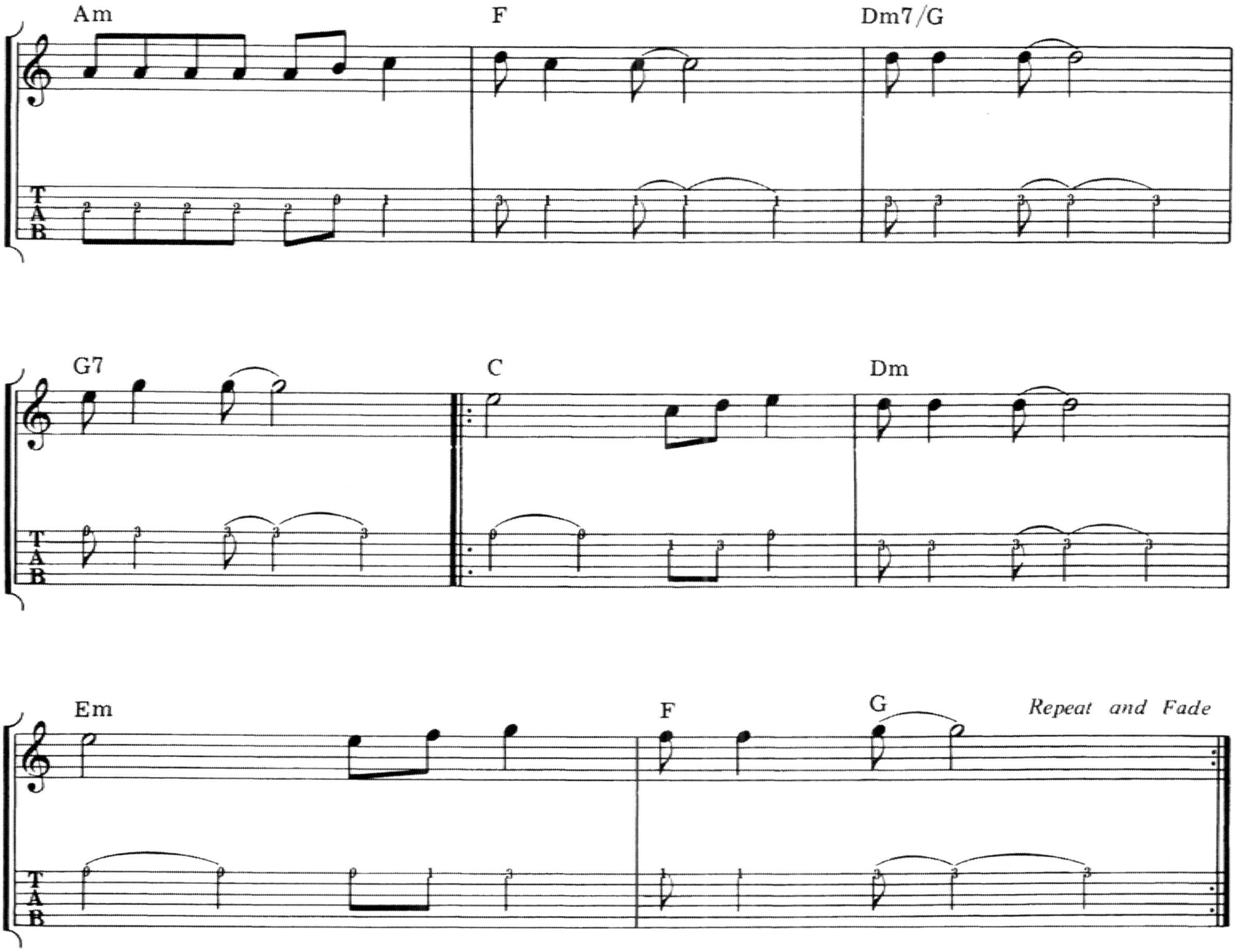


SUGGESTED STRUM: DRIVIN' - ROCK

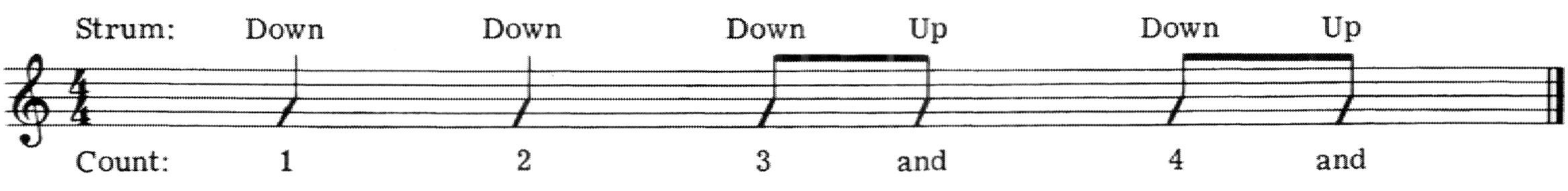


CHORDS USED:

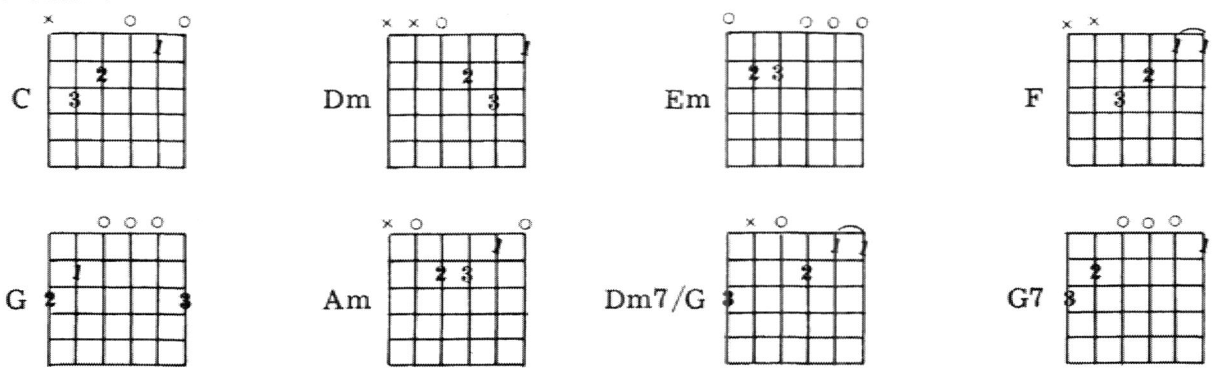

# BACK CREEK ROCK

SUGGESTED STRUM : FOLK ROCK

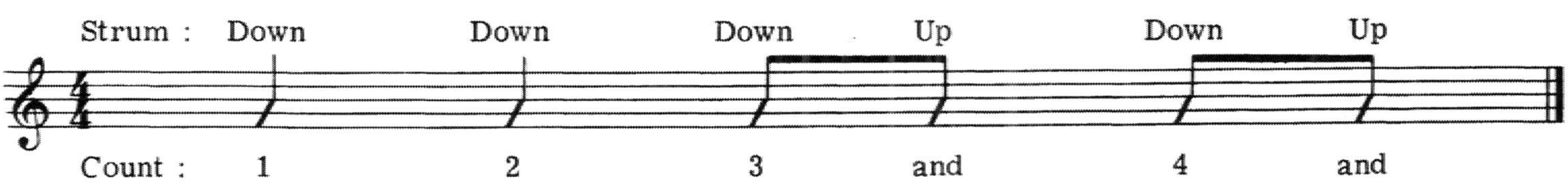


CHORDS USED :

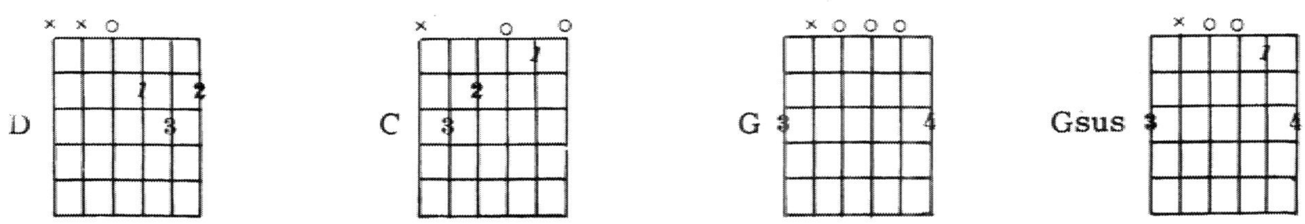

# BUMPIN' BAD

SUGGESTED STRUM : BUMP

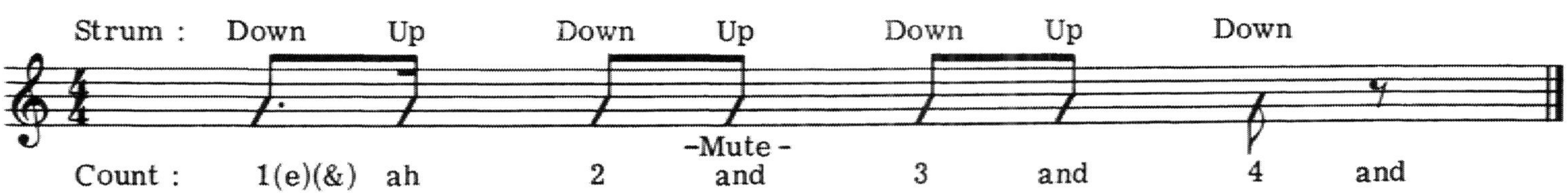


CHORDS USED :

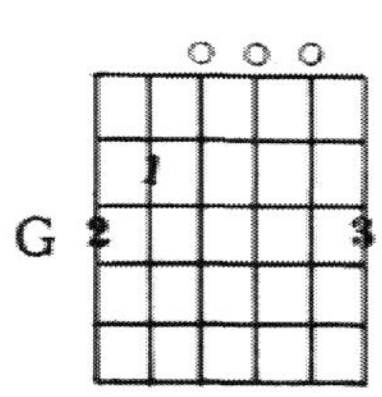


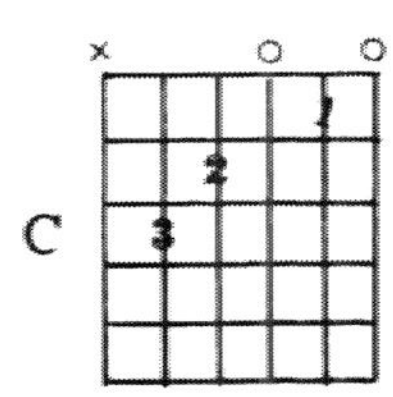


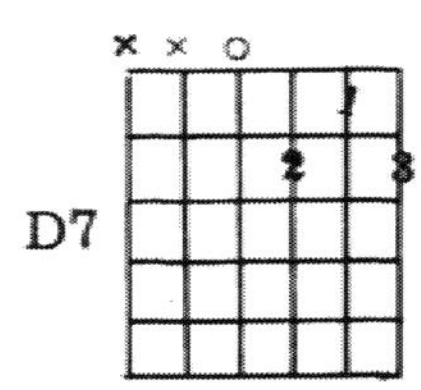

# FUNKY GROOVE

SUGGESTED STRUM : FUNKY

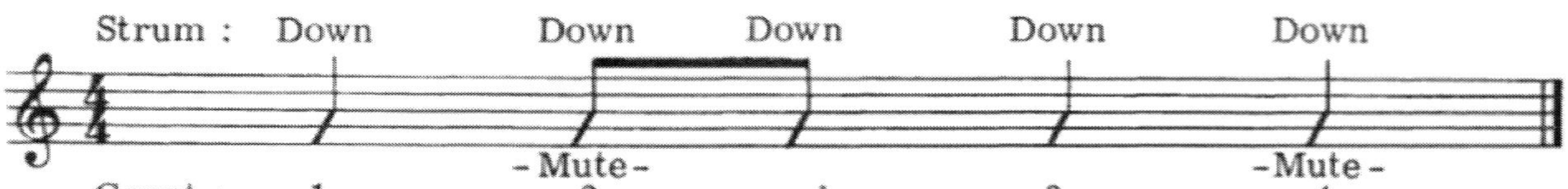


CHORDS USED :

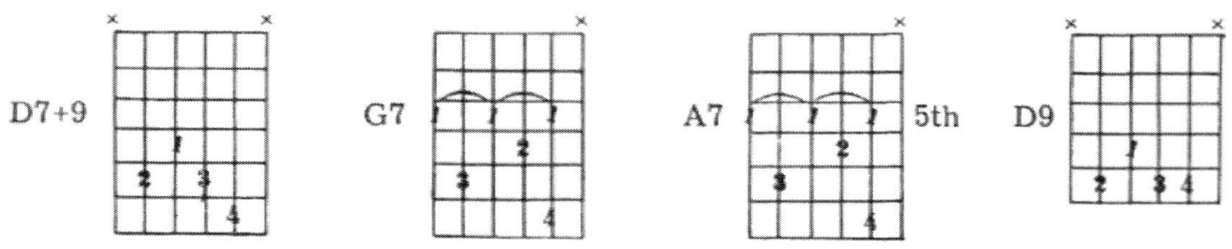

# The Texas Twister

# Easy Blues

Moderato
G C G C G C
G C C F C F
G C G C D A
D A C G C G
G C G C G C G C
Fingering simile
repeat and fade

# Blues in E

# Boogie Beat

# Chicken Gumbo

NOT a moveable form because of the open strings. Play in this key (G) only.

Gliss means to slide fingers to the 2 - 3 next fret. Play $\frac{2}{3}$ - slide to $\frac{3}{4}$
3 - 4

# Boogie Rock

Practise this pattern with down strokes: then, down-up strokes.

| FRET | 1 | 2 | 4 | 5 | 6 | 7 | 8 | 9 |
|---|---|---|---|---|---|---|---|---|
| KEYS | F | G♭ | G | A♭ | A | B♭ | C♭ | C |

# Bayou Blues

Strike grace notes at beginning of each measure and slide up to principal notes. Do NOT strike principal notes following grace notes. EXAMPLE: →

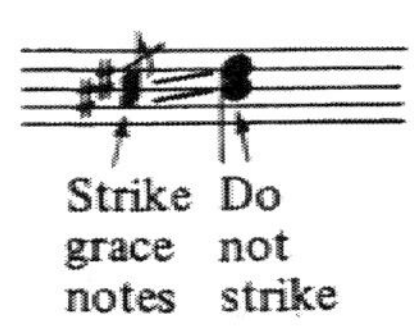


Practise in all keys shown in this chart. } → 

| FRET | 3 | 4 | 5 | 6 | 7 | 8 |
|---|---|---|---|---|---|---|
| KEY | G | A♭ | A | B♭ | C♭ | C |

# Delta Doll

Down strokes throughout this exercise.

X - Means hold finger down until forced to remove it.

# FINGERSTYLE SOLOS and COUNTRY BLUES SOLOS

# FINGERSTYLE SOLOS

## The Skaters

Expressive medium waltz

WALDTEUFEL
Arr. by Tommy Flint

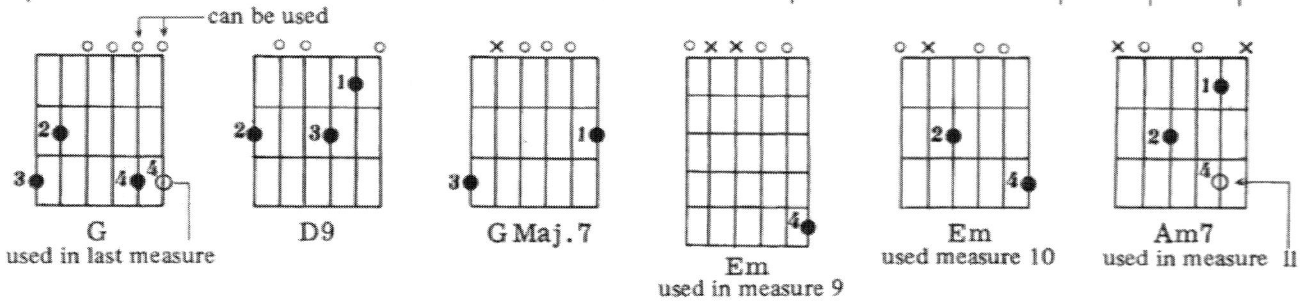

# Redbud Waltz

Tommy Flint

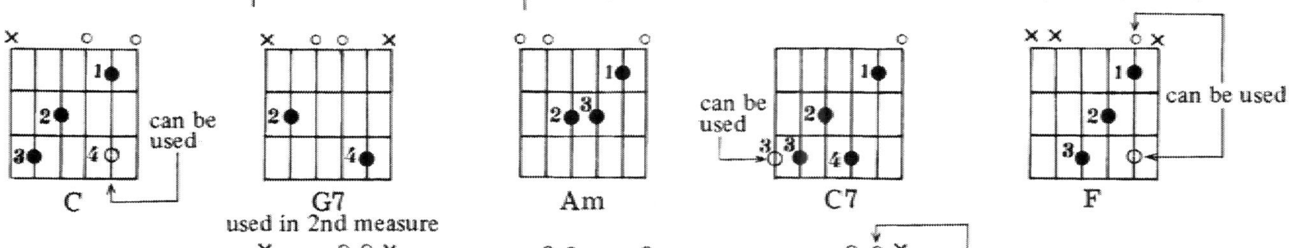


*Do not hold chord.
Play as written.

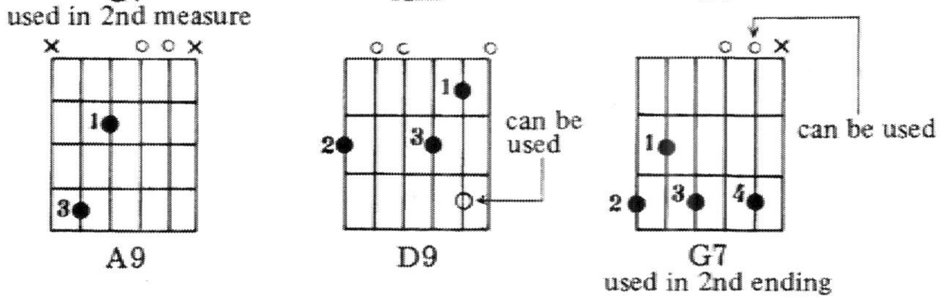

# Huron Cove

Tommy Flint

**Medium**

# Early Spring

Tommy Flint

**Moderate**

# Grandfather's Clock

Arr. Tommy Flint

C
D9
G7
C
G7
C
F
C
G7
C
F
C
F
C
G7

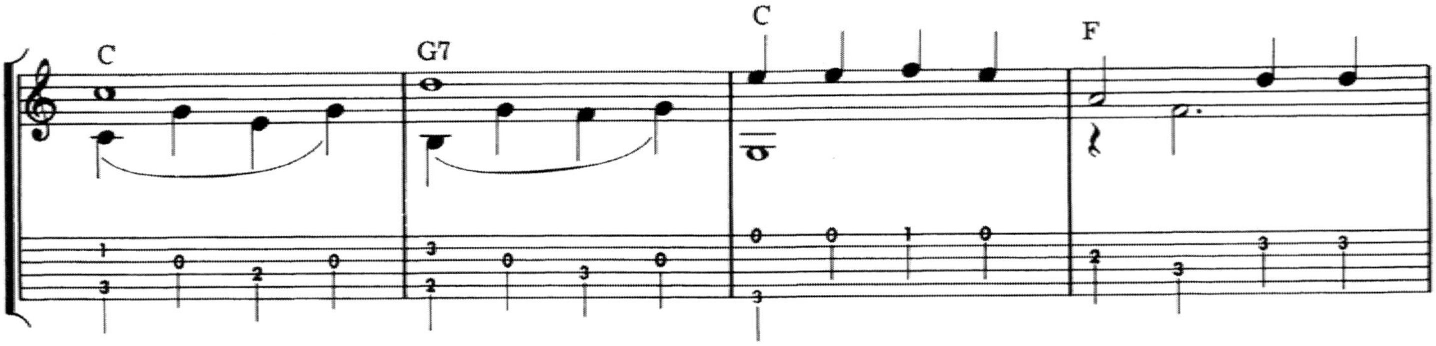
C
G7
C
F

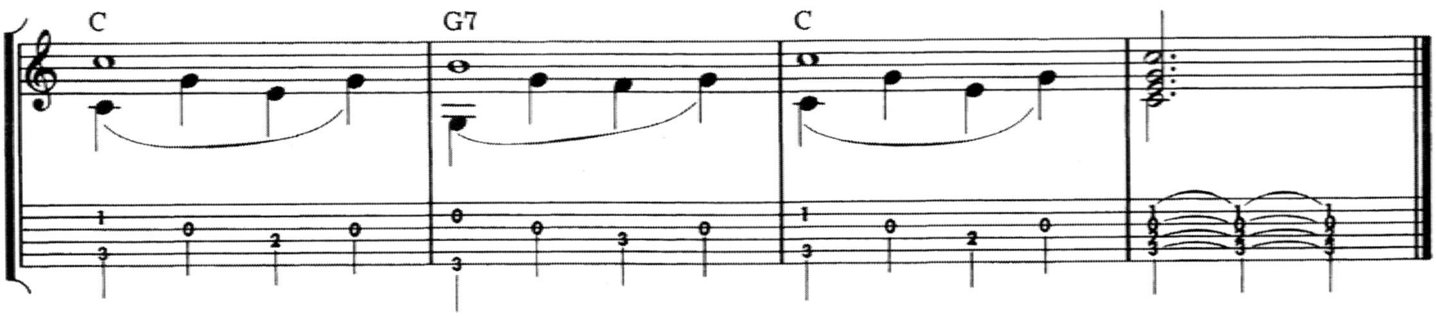
C
G7
C

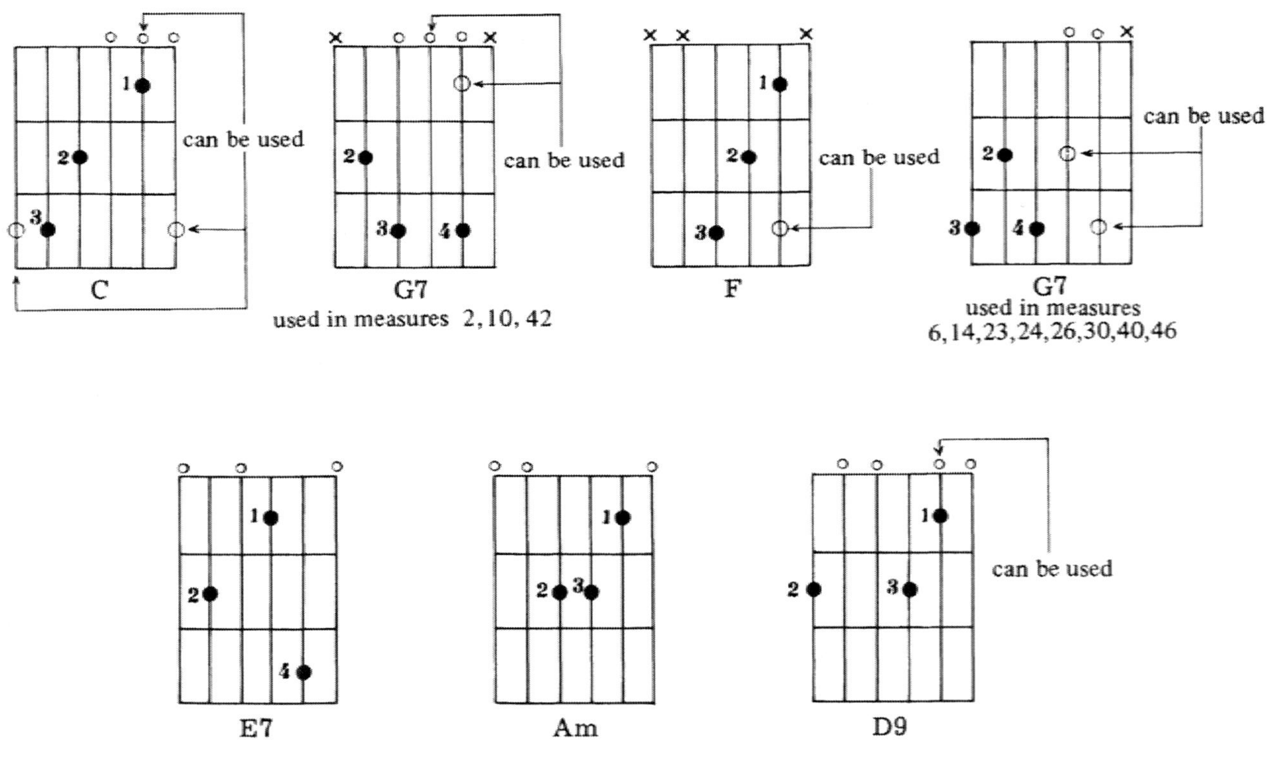
can be used
C
can be used
G7
used in measures 2, 10, 42
can be used
F
can be used
G7
used in measures
6, 14, 23, 24, 26, 30, 40, 46
E7
Am
can be used
D9

# The Hills of Brown

Tommy Flint

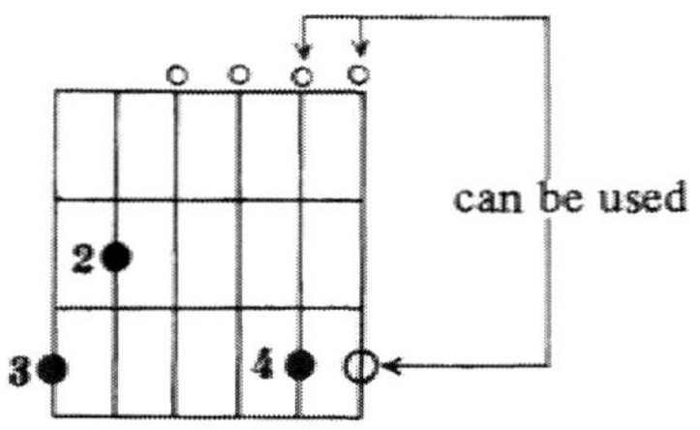


G

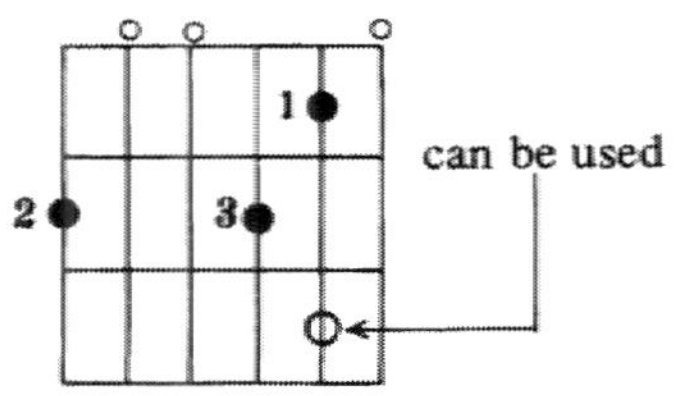


D9

# Knoxville Town

Tommy Flint

* Do not hold chord. Play notes or numbers as written.

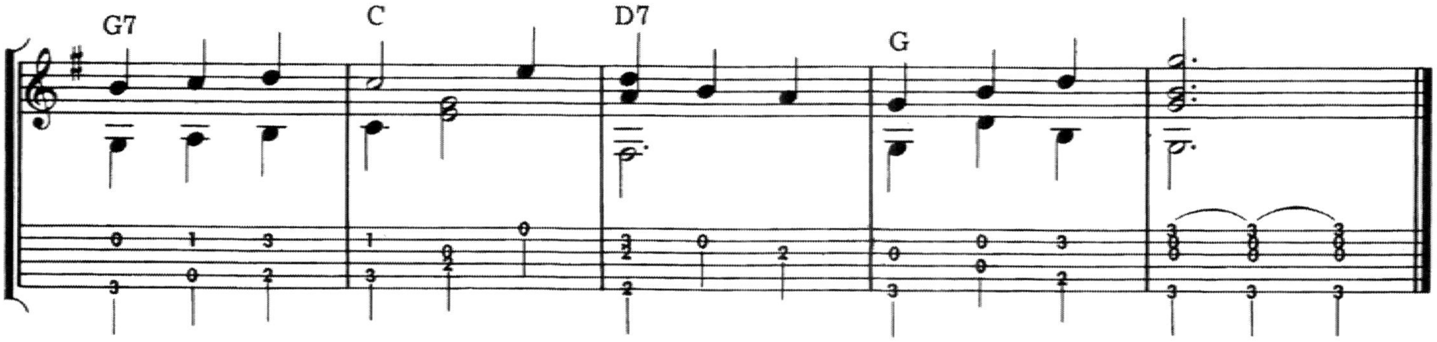


## The Chords Used in Knoxville Town

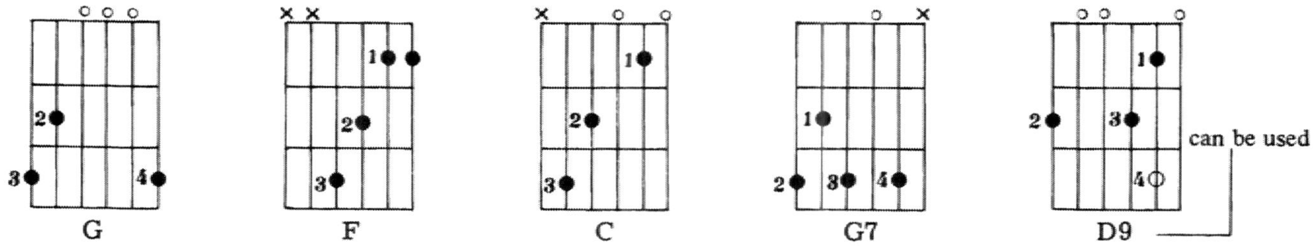


# I'm On My Way

Arr. Tommy Flint

# Green Grow the Lilacs

Arr. Tommy Flint

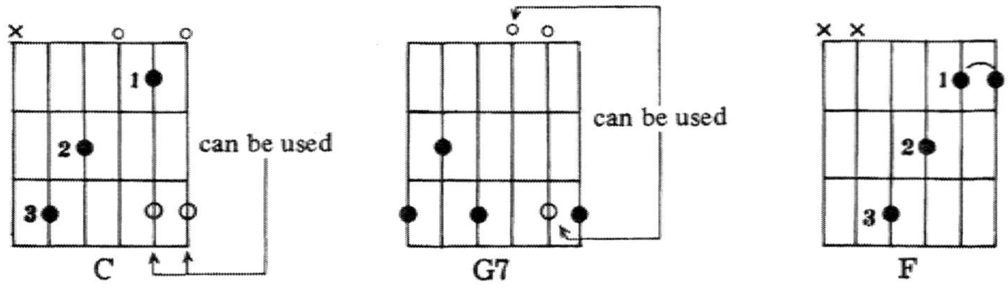


* Do not hold chord. Play single notes.

# The Carnival of Venice

**Moderately bright** — **Arr. Tommy Flint**

# FINGERSTYLE—COUNTRY BLUES SOLOS

## The Blues Every Night

In the following solo the thumb will play whole notes on the bass strings. The index and middle fingers will be used to play the melody line.

**Tommy Flint**

**Slow**

To create a slight variation place the finger one or two frets lower on the first string and slide into the first note in measures 1, 3, 5, 7 and 11.
The first and sixth strings are played simultaneously. The slide is very rapid.

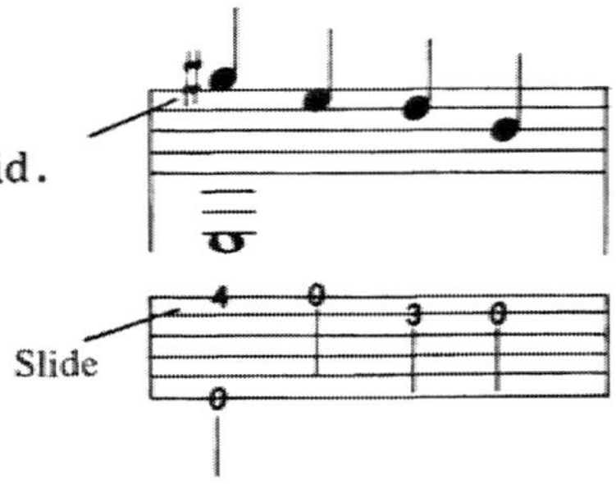


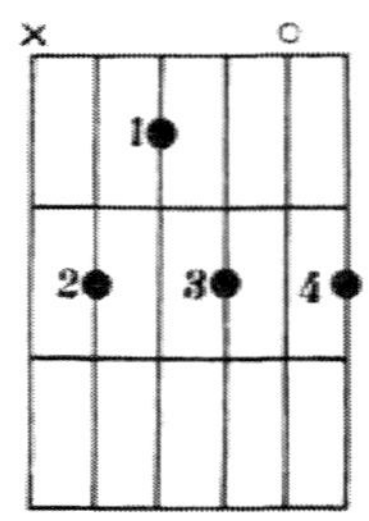

B7

# St. Joseph Island Blues

In this arrangement the thumb plays a two beat bass.
Again the index and middle fingers are used on the melody line.
Be sure to hold the chords.

**Medium**

**Tommy Flint**

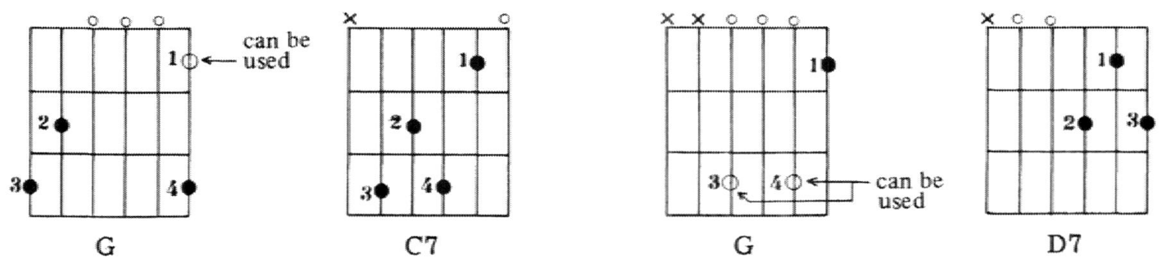

# Sunday Morning Blues
## A Sixteen Measure Blues Two Beat Bass

Tommy Flint

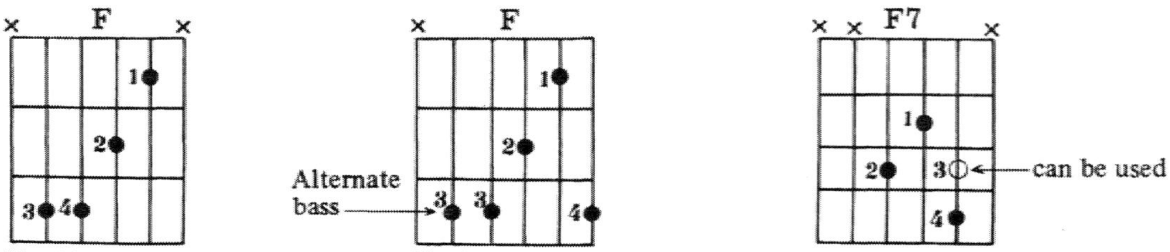


Used in measure number three

Used in measure number four

# Mississippi River Blues

Tommy Flint

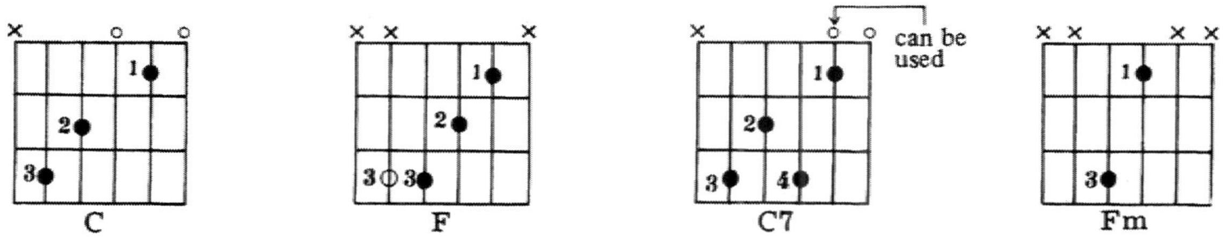


* Do not make a chord. sixth intervals.

# South Bound Blues

## A Sixteen Measure Blues

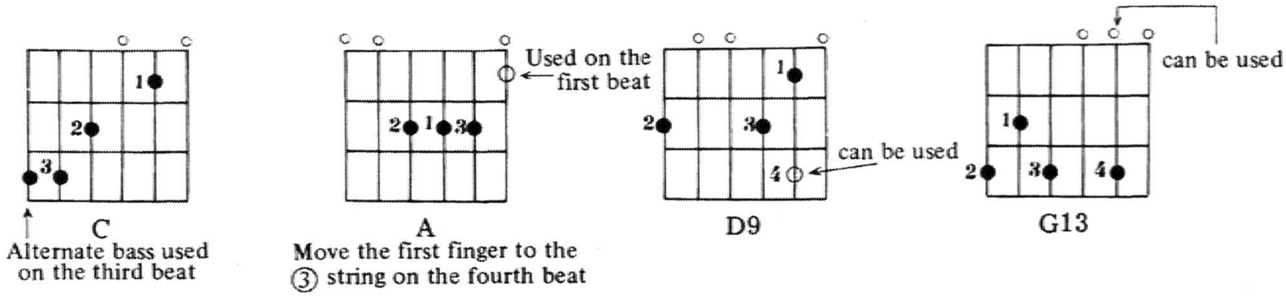

# Appalachian Twilight Blues

## Whole Note Basses

Tommy Flint

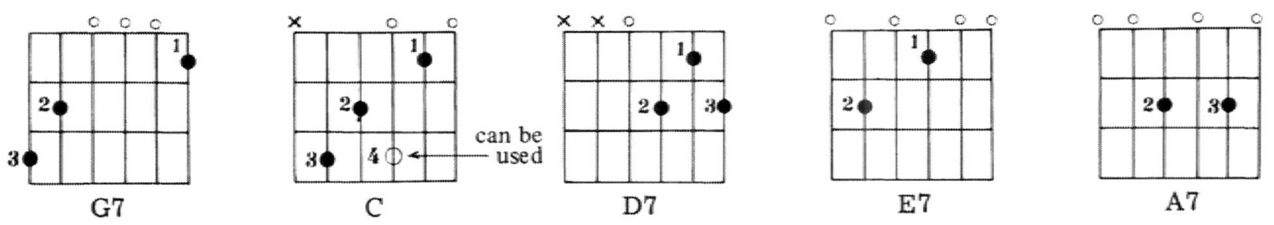

# Pay Day Blues

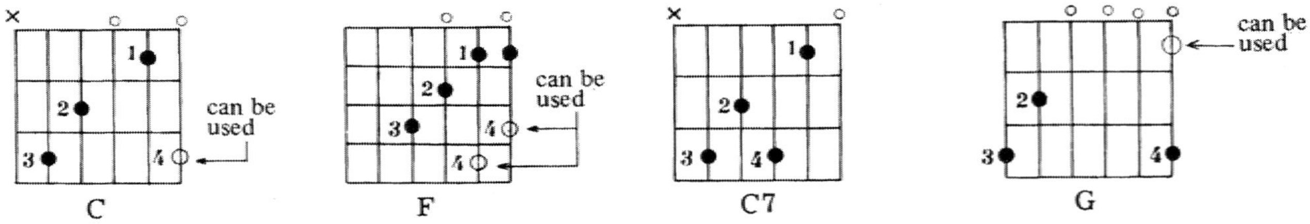


In this solo the basic chord should be held for the duration of the measure in which it is used. The fourth finger will be used for all additional notes except in G chord in which the first finger is used.

**Tommy Flint**

**Medium**

**Variation I**

F
C
C7
G
F
C
Variation II
F
C
C7
F
C
C7
G
F
C

# It Takes a Worried Man

## A Sixteen Measure Blues

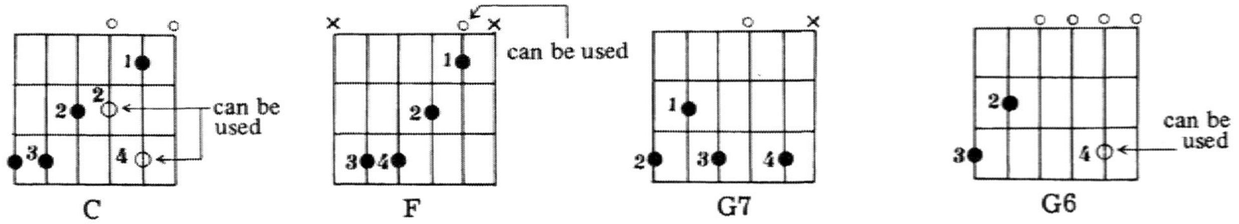


In measure number one while holding C chord lean the second finger over to play the A note on the fourth beat.

**Arr. Tommy Flint**

**Medium**

# Working at the Saw Mill Blues

Although the solo on this page is in the key of E there is no written key signature. This will somewhat facilitate the reading of the arrangement.

**Moderately slow** **Tommy Flint**

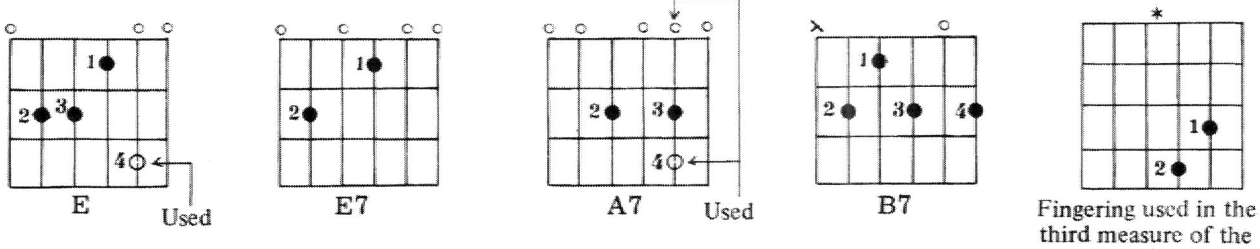


Fingering used in the third measure of the second ending

# Work Gang Blues

The bass note should be sustained or made to ring for the duration of the measure in which it is played. The B note will be played on the third string fourth fret unless indicated otherwise.

Tommy Flint

* The B note is played on the third string fourth fret.

# 12:04 Blues

The following solo is played with a slow triplet feel.

**Tommy Flint**

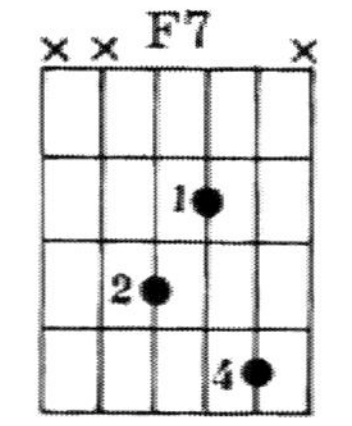


Used in measure number two

The E notes in measures number three and eleven are played on the second string fifth fret.

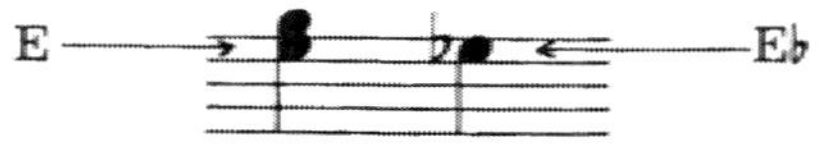


E♭ is on the second string fourth fret.

# NOTE READING
# and
# MELODIC DEVELOPMENT

The student should have completed the note Reading Section of Mel Bay's Guitar Class Method—Volume 1 or Mel Bay's Modern Guitar Method—Grade 1 before beginning this section

## THE NOTES ON THE FIRST STRING

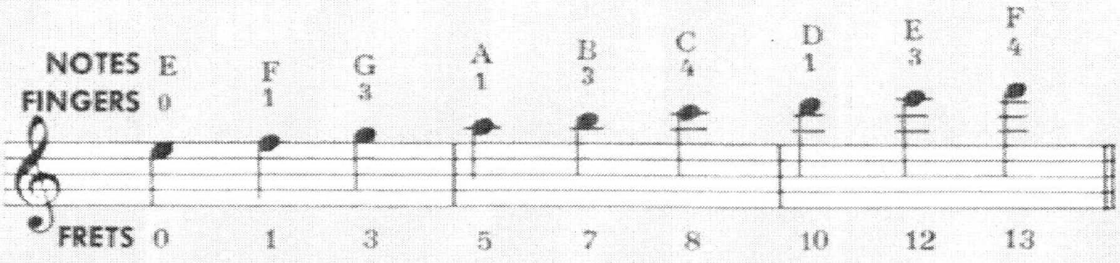


## SCALE OF C MAJOR

(Two Octaves)

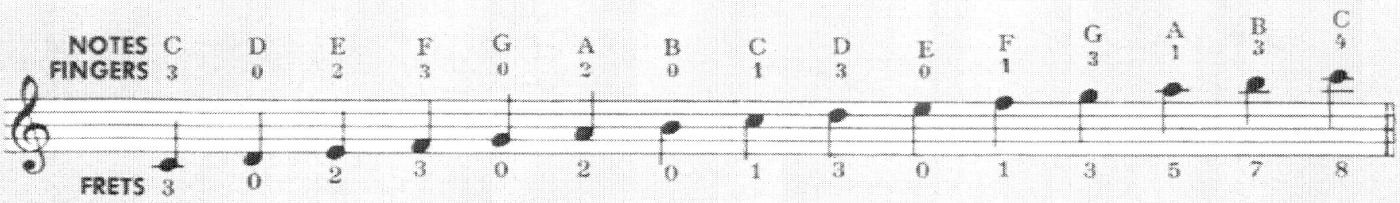


## A Rhythm Review

## Accompaniment For The Above Exercises

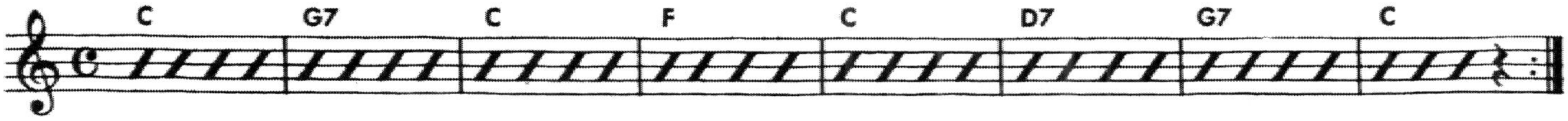

# Frolic

GUITAR DUET

Allegretto

Arr. by Mel Bay

# Senorita

GUITAR SOLO

Andante

CARCASSI-BAY

## Wade In The Water

Moderately

Spiritual

Accidentals are effective only in the measures in which they are found. When that measure is passed the accidentals become void.

In the following solo "THE GAUCHOS," the third part is in the key of C which explains the natural on the fifth line in the signature.

## The Gauchos

GUITAR SOLO

Allegro

CARCASSI-BAY

## The Little Prince

GUITAR DUET

MAZAS,
Arr. by Mel Bay

## Carry Me Back To Old Virginny

GUITAR SOLO

BLAND
Arr. by Mel Bay

*The wavy line before the last chord means to glide the pick slowly over the strings producing a harp-like effect. The musical term for this is QUASI ARPI.

# Maytime

GUITAR DUET

WANHALL-BAY

## TONE

Music is composed of sounds pleasant to the ear.

SOUND may be made from NOISE or TONE.

NOISE is made by **irregular vibrations** such as would be caused by striking a table with a hammer, the shot of a gun, or slapping two stones together.

TONE is produced by **regular vibrations** as would be caused by drawing a bow over the strings of a violin, striking the strings of a guitar, or blowing through a wind instrument, such as a trumpet.

A TONE has four characteristics . . . PITCH, DURATION, DYNAMICS and TIMBRE.

PITCH: The highness or lowness of a tone.

DURATION: The length of a tone.

DYNAMICS The force or power of a tone. (Loudness or softness).

TIMBRE: Quality of the tone.

A NOTE represents the PITCH AND DURATION of a tone.

DYNAMICS are indicated by words such as . . .

| | | |
|---|---|---|
| Pianissimo | (*pp*) | Very soft |
| Piano | (*p*) | Soft |
| Mezzo piano | (*mp*) | Medium soft |
| Mezzo forte | (*mf*) | Medium loud |
| Forte | (*f*) | Very loud |

TIMBRE depends upon the skill of the performer plus the quality of the instrument on which he is playing.

# Rondo

**GUITAR DUET**

**MAZAS, Op. 85**
**Arr. by Mel Bay**

Allegro

Student should
play both parts

## Sor's Waltz

Arr. by Mel Bay

## Bluegrass Waltz

## Running the Thirds in G

## A Little Bit of Hanon

## Southern Fried

# ALTERNATE PICKING

One of the most difficult things for the student is the mastery of the alternate stroke on diatonic passages.

To promote greater speed with proper accentation, the alternate stroke should be developed.

The following study will seem difficult at first but by practicing slowly, placing the down-strokes on the beats, followed by an up-stroke, the desired result will be accomplished.

## Etude

## The Hope

**(Hatikvoh)**

Hebrew Song

# Leapfrog

GUITAR DUET

Arr. by Mel Bay

Allegro

## How To Count Triplets

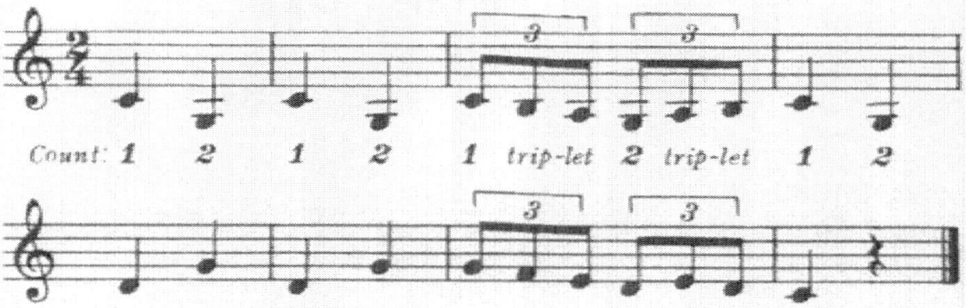


**Q.** What are TRIPLETS?

**A.** A group of three notes, played in the time of two notes of the same kind.

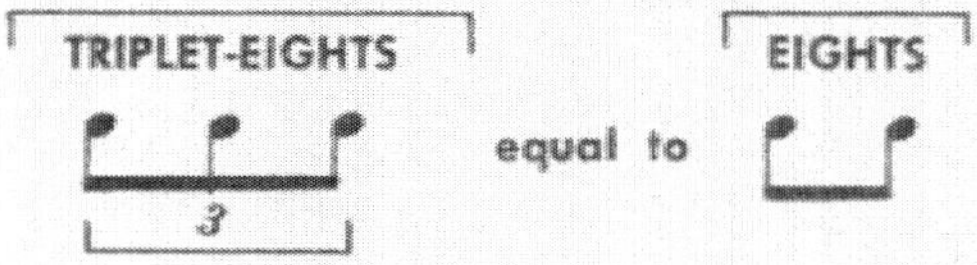


## Tarantelle

Moderato

## A Triple Play

GUITAR SOLO

Moderato

MEL BAY

# Triplet Duet

Pupil to practice both parts.

# Barcelona

BILL BAY

# THE KEY OF F

The Key of F will have one flat. All B-notes will be played one half-step lower as shown.

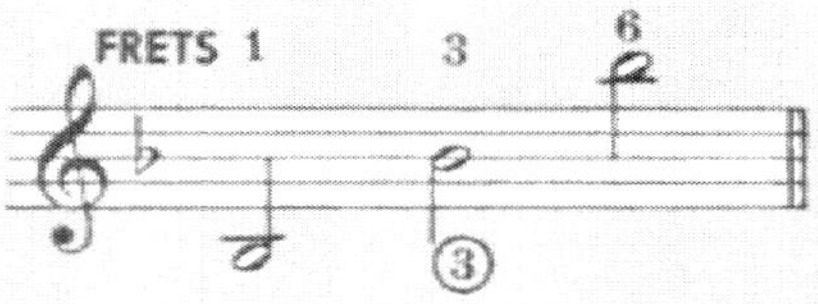


## THE F MAJOR SCALE
(Two Octaves)

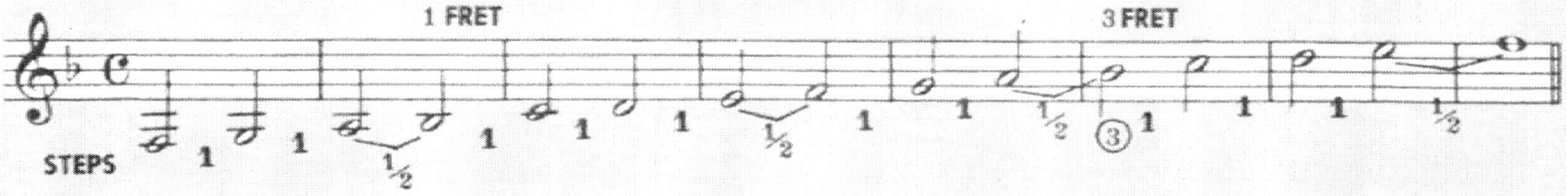


Practice the following exercise using the down-stroke throughout.
Later on use the alternate stroking shown.

## A Daily Study

## March Majestic

GUITAR SOLO

Arr. by Mel Bay

**D. S. al Fine (Dal Segno al Fine)** Go back to the sign 𝄋 and play to **Fine** the end).

## THE CHORDS IN THE KEY OF F

The three chords in the key of F are F, B-flat, and C7.

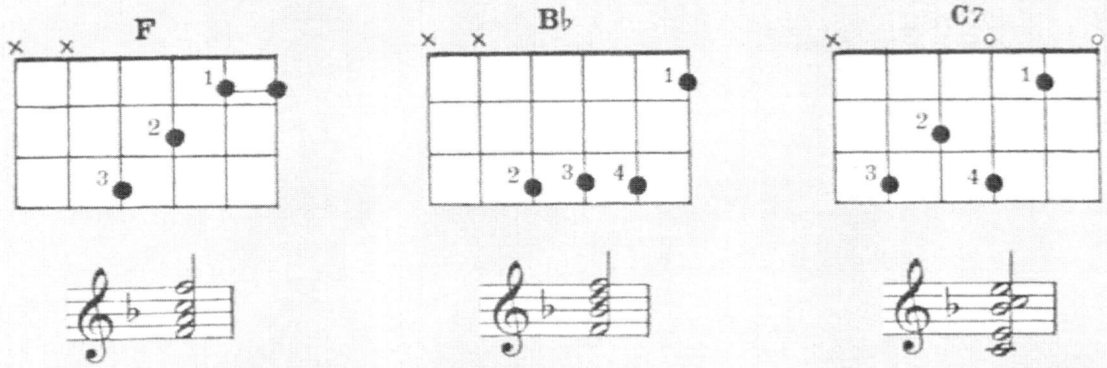


## Accompaniment Styles

### Common Time

### Three-Four Time

### Two-Four Time

## Melody In F

GUITAR SOLO

RUBENSTEIN-BAY

## MUSICAL TERMS

**ANIMATO** — Lively

**CANTABILE** — In a singing style

**SFORZANDO** — (*sfz*) — Forcing the tone suddenly loud.

**MORENDO** — Dying or fading away.

**AD LIBITUM** — (A Piacere) — At the liberty of the performer.

**A TEMPO** — Back to the regular tempo.

**CRESCENDO** (cresc.) — Gradually grow louder.

**DIMINUENDO** (dim.) — Gradually grow softer.

**DOLCE** — Sweetly

**MAESTOSO** — Majestic

**PIU MOSSO** — Quicker

**SOSTENUTO** — Sustained

GUITAR DUET

# I Love Thee

**(Duet)**

Christian Hymn

# TETRACHORDS

A TETRACHORD is a four tone scale arranged in the following sequence:

**WHOLE-STEP, WHOLE-STEP, HALF-STEP** $(1, 1, \frac{1}{2})$

Each major scale is made up of two tetrachords as shown in the example:

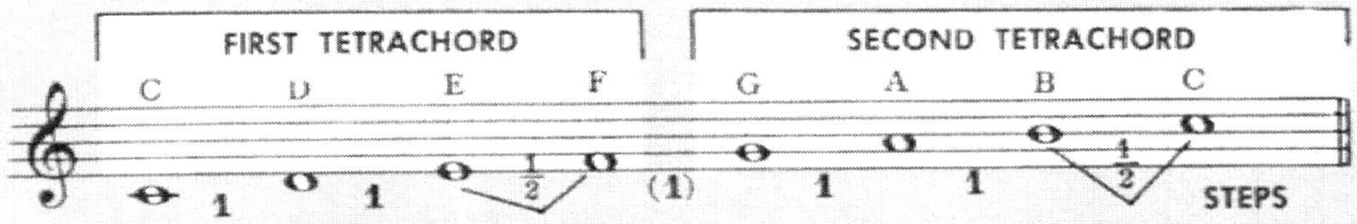


The two tetrachords in the major scales are separated by one whole-step.

# RELATED KEYS

The first tetrachord of the C scale will be the last tetrachord of the F scale and the second tetrachord becomes the first one in the G scale.

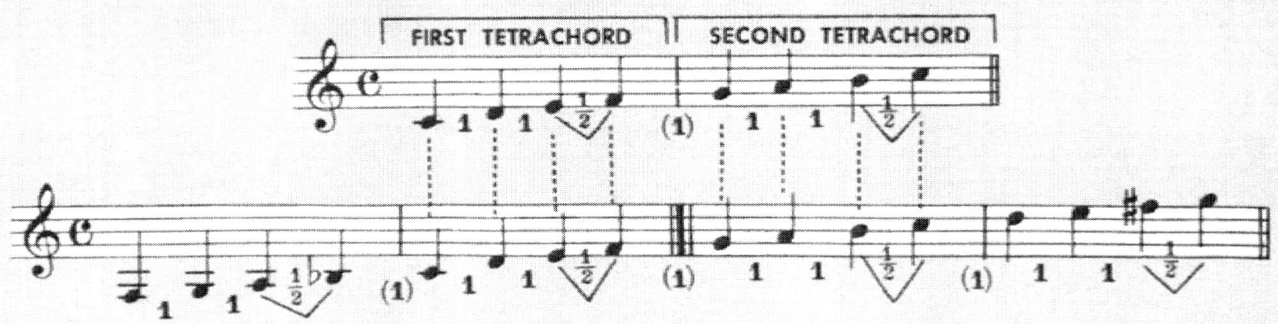


# THE TECHNICAL NAMES OF THE SCALE STEPS

Each degree of the scale will be designated by a number and a specific technical name. Up to this point in this course we have referred only to the letter name of each degree depending on the note falling on each degree. The number of each scale degree will be in Roman numerals.

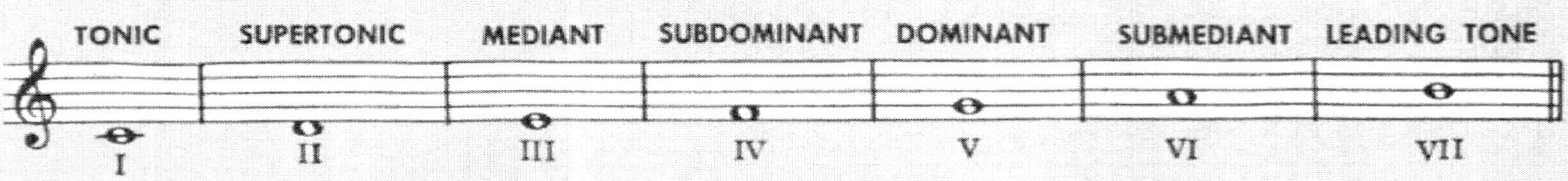


# THE CHROMATIC SCALE

The Chromatic Scale is composed of **twelve half-steps** within an octave.

It may be written from pitch; the Key-Signature will be that of the Major Key of the chosen pitch. It is written upward in sharps and downward in flats..

## INTERVALS

An INTERVAL is the distance between two tones or the difference in pitch between two tones when sounded.

Intervals are measured **upward** from the lower tone to the higher.

Intervals have NUMBER names and TYPE names. For example a 3rd could be majjor or minor depending upon the distance.

The staff degree occupied by the lower note and the staff degree occupied by the higher note are **both included** when determining the number name of the interval.

Below are nine intervals from C to each note in the C scale.

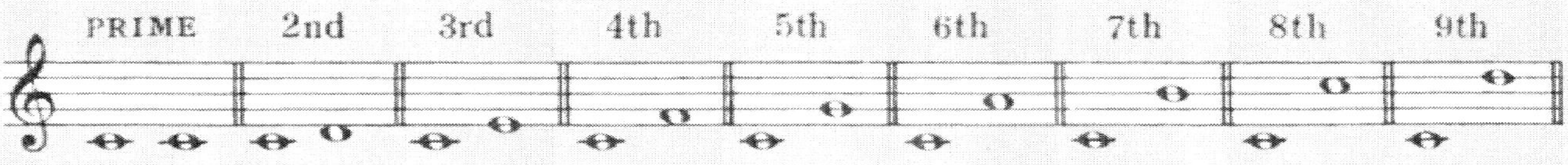


The TYPES of intervals will be discussed later.

## A Daily Study In F

In the following Solo "The Carousel" the second part is in the Key of C.

The first line is repeated and after the second line is played, the first line played only once ending at FINE. This will give the solo a total of 32 measures.

It should be practiced slowly at first and continued until a gay spirited tempo is attained.

## The Carousel

**GUITAR SOLO**

**MEL BAY**

# The Recital

**GUITAR DUET**

**MAZAS**

**Arr. by Mel Bay**

# Triplet Etude

All down-stroke.

# The Happy Farmer

**GUITAR SOLO**

**ROBERT SCHUMANN**
**(Op. 68, No. 10)**
**Arr. by Mel Bay**

Allegretto

# THE KEY OF D MINOR

(Relative to F Major)

## The D Minor Scales

HARMONIC

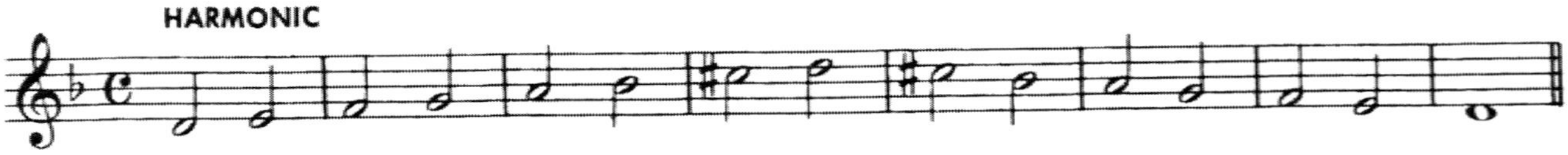

MELODIC

## Etude In D Minor

HARMONIC

MELODIC

## March Slav

GUITAR SOLO

TSCHAIKOWSKY

Arr. by Mel Bay

Slow

## THE CHORDS IN THE KEY OF D MINOR

The three principal chords in the key of D minor are:

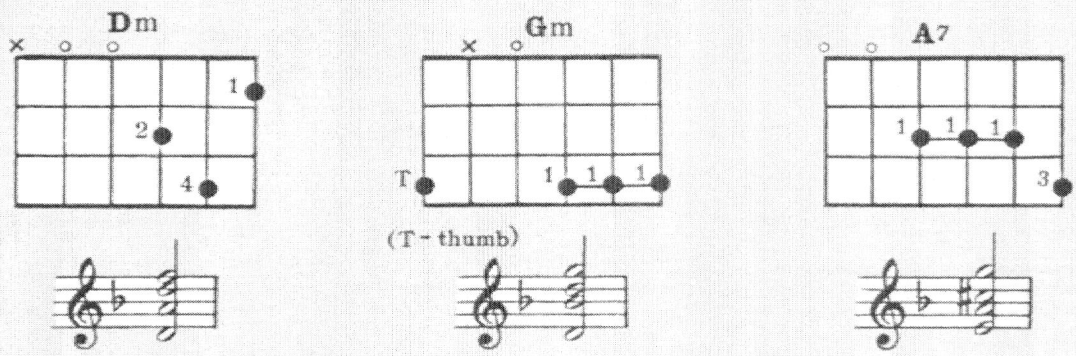


## Accompaniment Styles

### Common Time

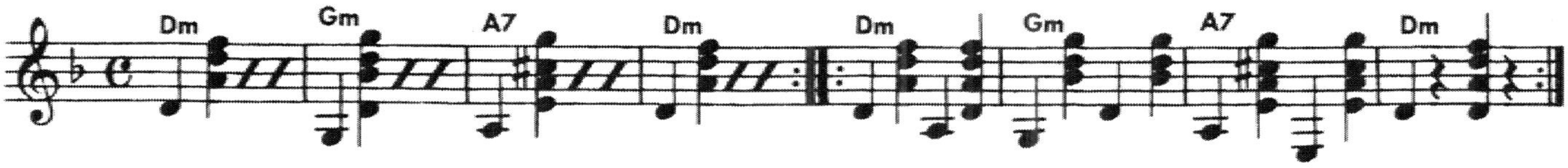


### Three-Four Time

### Two-Four Time

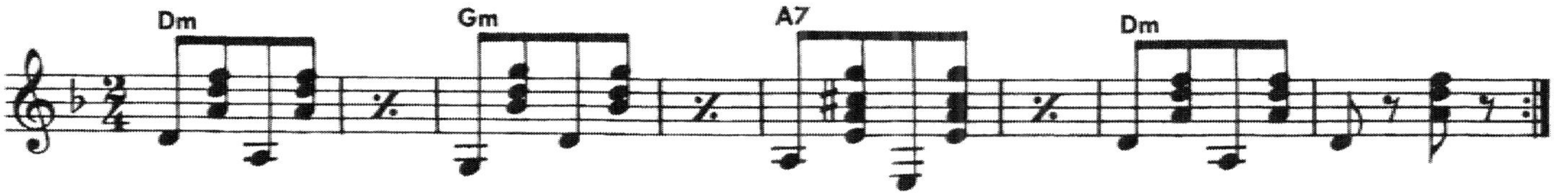


**EXAMPLE:**

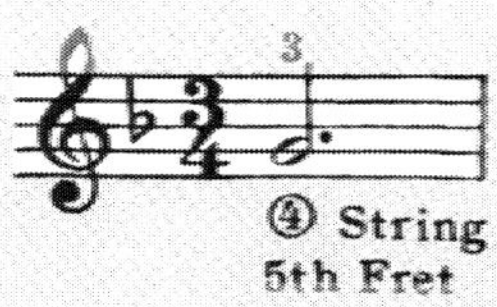


In the fifth and seventh measures of the guitar solo "BALKAN MOON" the note G will be played as shown in the example:

Place the third finger upon the fourth string behind the fifth fret.

## Balkan Moon

GUITAR SOLO

MEL BAY

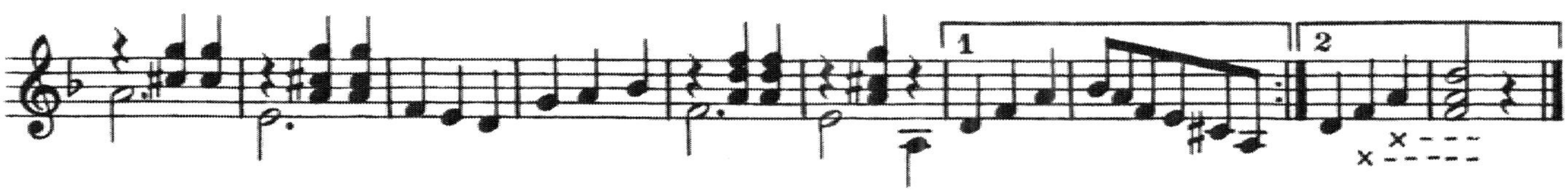

# FINGER GYMNASTICS

The following exercises have a two-fold purpose.

(1) Training the individual fingers to perform independently of each other.

(2) Acquainting the student with the technic of position playing that will be an important part of this course.

The first finger should be held down throughout these exercises.

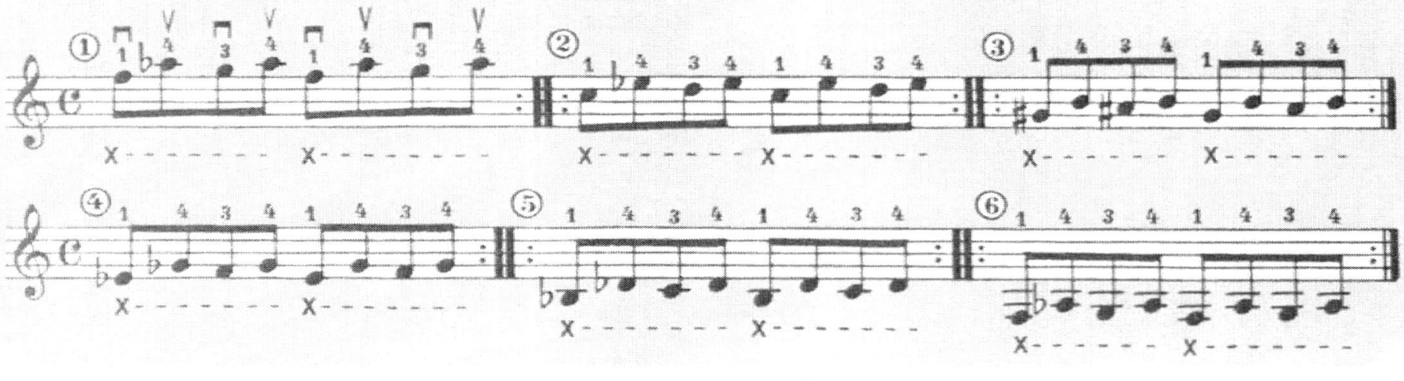

## Duet In D Minor

**GUITAR DUET**

**MAZAS**
**Arr. by Mel Bay**

## THE NOTES ON THE SECOND STRING

Shown below are the notes on the second string.

Any note played upon the first string may be played upon the second string **five frets higher** than it's location on the first string.

In the following diagram you will see the notes on the first string and directly below the same notes as played upon the second string. This is a very good aid in remembering the notes on the second string.

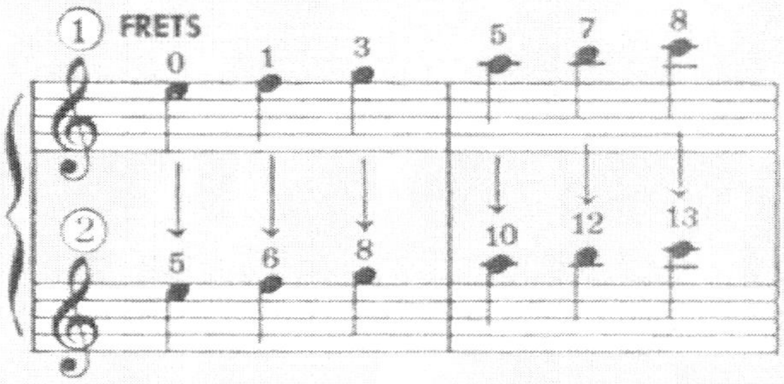


## THE C SCALE IN THIRDS

The following study should be played upon the first and second strings.

The **top-note will be on the first string** and the **bottom-note on the second.**

To facilitate execution, it is better to let the fingers remain upon the strings as much as possible, gliding from fret to fret.

Carefully observe the fingering.

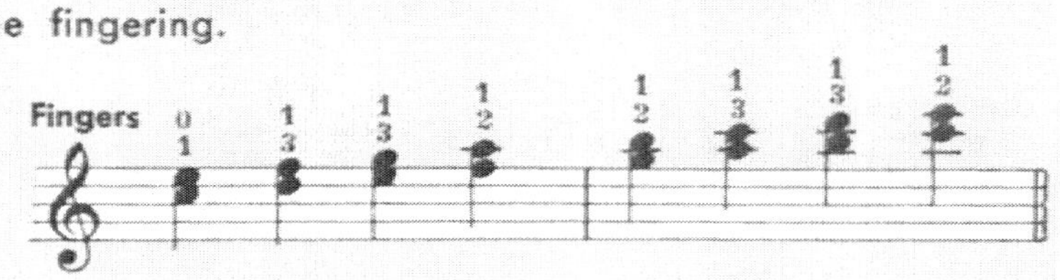


## An Exercise In Thirds

# THE NOTES ON THE FIFTH FRET

# THE THIRDS IN THE KEY OF G

## Granada Memories

GUITAR SOLO

(Based upon an etude by Aguado)

Moderato

MEL BAY

# THE MAJOR CHORD

The Major Chord is formed by combining the first, third and fifth tones of the major scale.

The first tone of the scale will be known as the **root** of the chord.

The Major Chord may be arranged in three positions called Inversions.

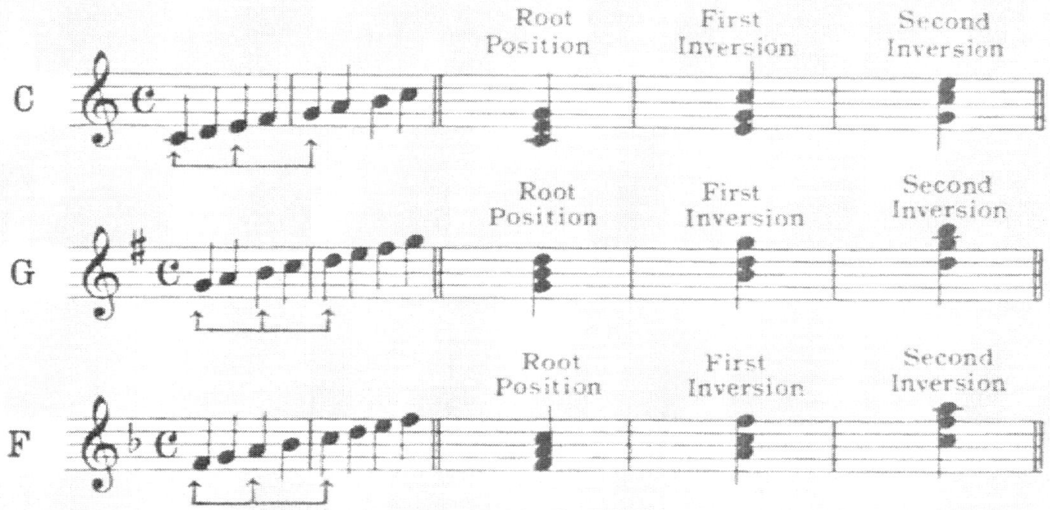


# THIRDS IN THE KEY OF F

**GUITAR SOLO**

## Juanita

Moderato

Arr. by Mel Bay

## Santa Lucia

GUITAR DUET

Arr. by Mel Bay

Moderato

## Swing Low Sweet Chariot

Slowly

Spiritual

## Dolores

WALDTEUFEL, Op. 170
Arr. by Mel Bay

Andantino

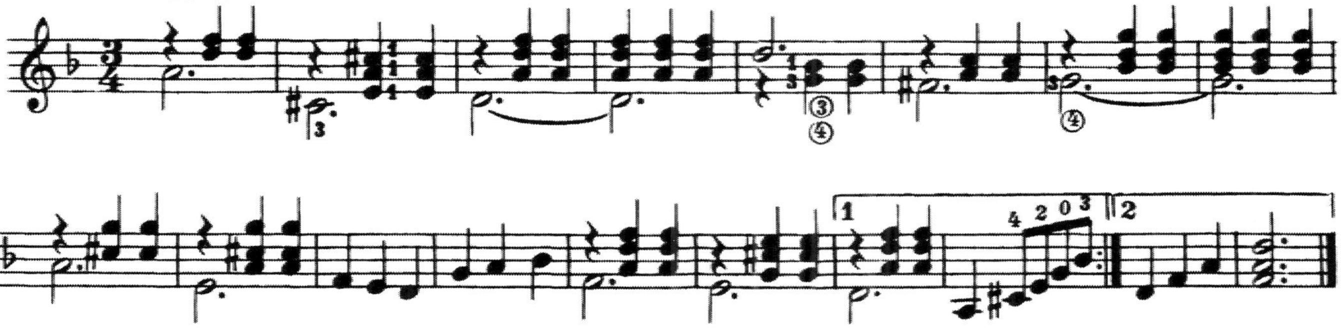

GUITAR DUET

## Romance

MAZAS
Arr. by MEL BAY

Andante

# Trail Ridge

**GUITAR DUET**

Andante

Arr. by Mel Bay

# Manitou

Moderato

# Mesa Verde

Moderato

# Were You There?

Spiritual

# Now The Day Is Over

Slowly (Duet) Hymn

# Sonatina

**GUITAR DUET**

**MAZAS**
**Arr. by Mel Bay**

Andante

# THE KEY OF D MAJOR

The Key of D Major will have two sharps—F♯ and C♯.

To facilitate the fingering in the Key of D Major, it is necessary to move the first finger to the second fret, the second finger to the third fret and the third finger to the fourth fret.
(Note scale)

## THE D MAJOR SCALE

## Exercise

## THE CHORDS IN THE KEY OF D MAJOR

The chords in D Major are D, G and A7.

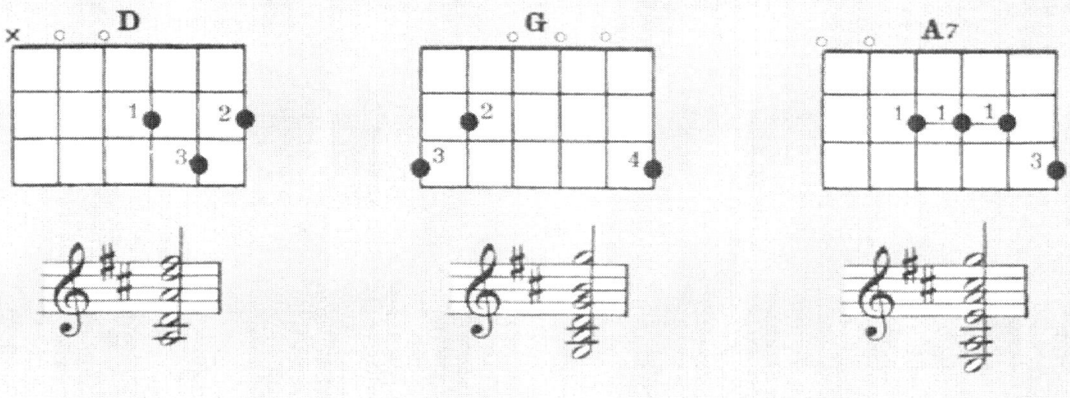


## Accompaniment Styles

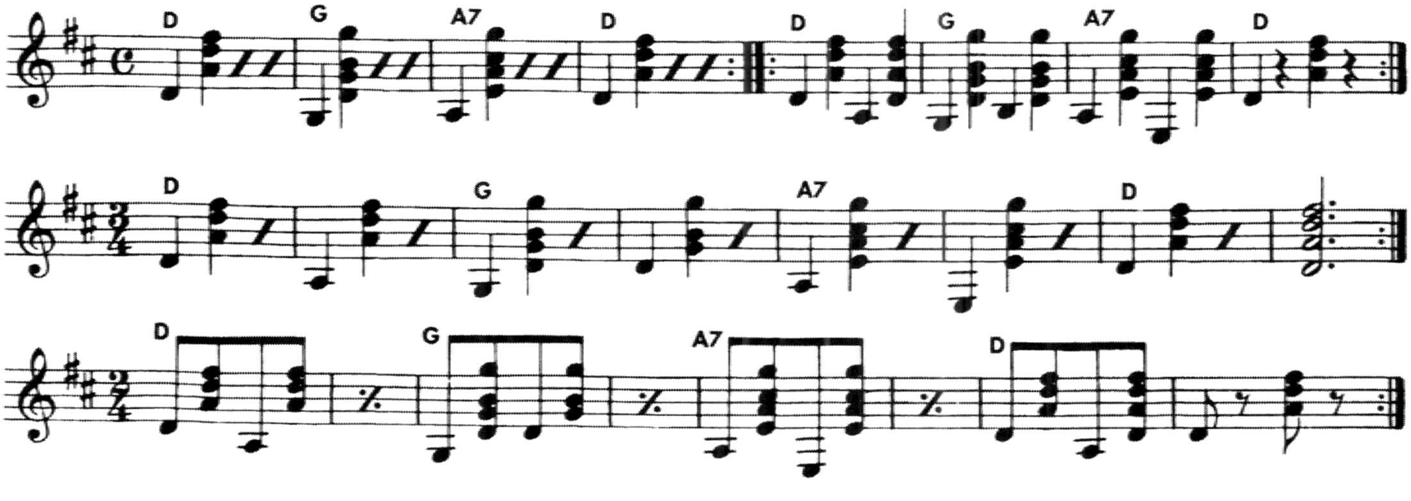

# Rondo

**GUITAR DUET**

**M. GEBAUER, Opus 10**
**Arr. by Mel Bay**

Allegretto

# THE D SCALE IN TWO OCTAVES

## Exercise

## Cielito Lindo

GUITAR SOLO

Arr. by Mel Bay

# THE SECOND POSITION

The SECOND POSITION extends from the second to the fifth frets.

In the SECOND POSITION:

The first finger will cover the second fret.

The second finger will cover the third fret.

The third finger will cover the fourth fret.

The fourth finger will cover the fifth fret.

## Notes in the Second Position

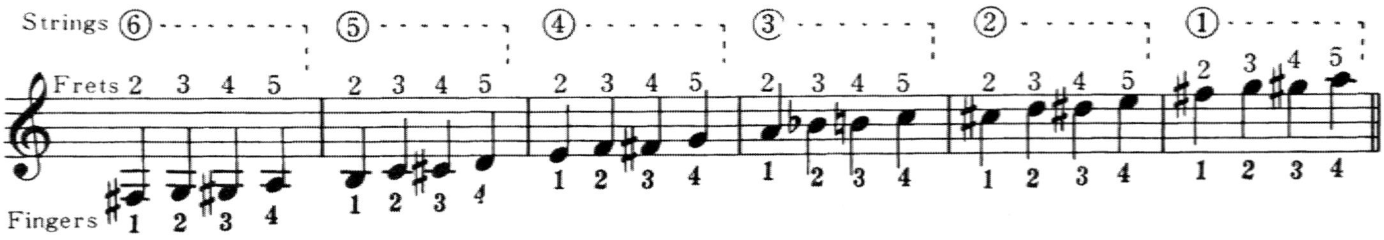


When practicing the position studies that follow it is important that you use the fingering as indicated above.

The major keys played in the Second position are G, D, and A.

There will be **no open strings.**

## Complete Scale of D Major in Second Position

## Second Position Etude No. 1

## Second Position Etude Number One (Key of D)

## He's Got The Whole World In His Hands

(Second Position)

# THIRDS IN THE KEY OF D

GUITAR SOLO

## Drink To Me Only With Thine Eyes

Arr. by Mel Bay

GUITAR DUET

## Caprice

MAZAS, Opus 38
Arr. by Mel Bay

The following selections will be played entirely in the second position. Please observe fingering.

## Turkey In The Straw

(Second Position)

## Soldiers' Joy

(Second Position)

# Minuet In D

**GUITAR DUET**

Arr. by Mel Bay

# SIXTEENTH-NOTES

In common time four sixteenth-notes equal one quarter-note.

They may be counted in this manner:

**1-six-teenth-notes, 2-six-teenth-notes, 3-six-teenth-notes, 4-six-teenth-notes.**

## Example

## TABLE OF NOTES AND RESTS

| Notes | Rests |
|---|---|
| Whole Note | A Whole Measure Rest |
| Half Notes | A Half Rest |
| Quarter Notes | A Quarter Rest |
| Eighth Notes | An Eighth Rest |
| Sixteenth Notes | A Sixteenth Rest |

In the fifth and ninth measures of the following study an eighth note is followed by two sixteenth notes.

They may be counted in this manner:

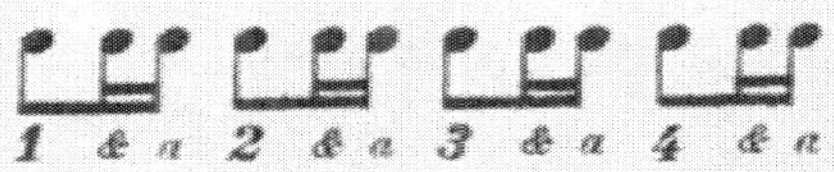


# A Speed Study In D

**(Second Position)**

Allegro

# THE KEY OF B MINOR

(Relative to D Major)

## THE B MINOR SCALES

## Etude In B Minor

## Aura Lee

GUITAR SOLO

Arr. by Mel Bay

# THE CHORDS IN THE KEY OF B MINOR

The chords in the key of B Minor are Bm, Em, and F♯7.

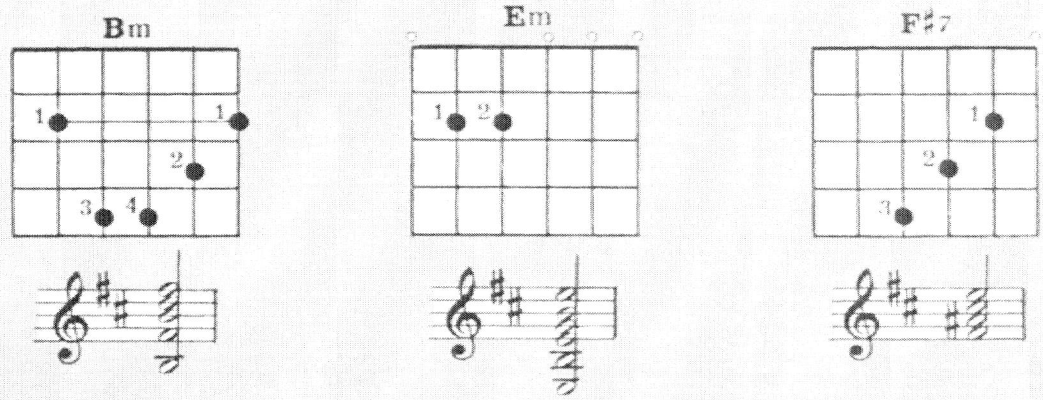


## Accompaniment Styles

GUITAR SOLO

## Waltz In B Minor

Andante

MEL BAY

# Duet In B Minor

GUITAR DUET

GEBAUER-BAY

## THE TECHNICAL NAMES OF THE CHORDS

As we learned on page 13, each degree of the scale has a technical name.

Chords built upon a scale degree will bear the technical name of that degree.

The three principal chords in any key are the TONIC, SUB-DOMINANT, and the DOMINANT-SEVENTH.

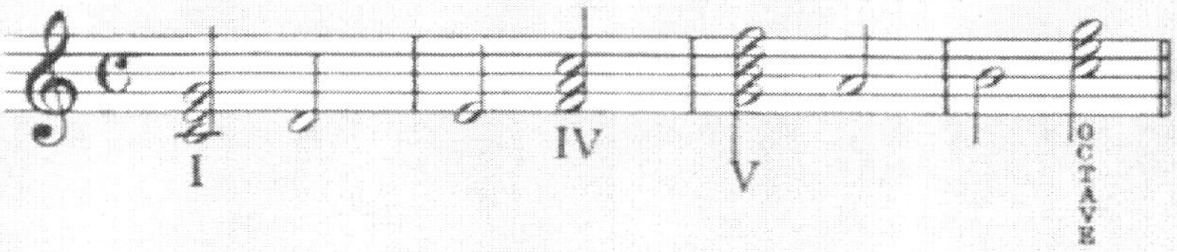


Note that the chords are built upon the Tonic, Sub-Dominant and Dominant degrees of the scale.

The lowest tone of a chord is called the ROOT and the remaining tones are numbered according to their distance from that root.

## SIX-EIGHT TIME

This sign  indicates six-eight time.

6 — beats per measure
8 — type of note receiving one beat

An Eighth-note ♪ = one beat, a quarter-note ♩ = two beats and a dotted quarter note ♩. = three beats, a sixteenth-note 𝅘𝅥𝅯 = ½ beat.

Six-eight time consists of two units containing three beats each.

It will be counted:  with the accents on beats one and four.

## The Irish Washerwomen

**GUITAR SOLO**

Arr. by MEL BAY

# PLECTRUM TECHNIC

## EIGHTH-NOTES

## TRIPLETS

## SIXTEENTH-NOTES

GUITAR SOLO

## Italian Waltz

CARULLI-BAY

# Minuet

**GUITAR DUET**

J. S. BACH
Arr. by Mel Bay

Andante

## THREE-EIGHT TIME

This sign  indicates three-eight time.

3 -- beats per measure.

8 -- type of note receiving one beat. (eight note)

An eighth-note = one beat, a quarter-note = two beats and a dotted quarter-note = three beats. A sixteenth-note = $\frac{1}{2}$ beat.

# A Spanish Dance

**GUITAR DUET**

**Arr. by Mel Bay**

# A Spanish Dance (cont.)

# PLECTRUM TECHNIC

The following studies are excellent for the development of plectrum technic.
Follow the stroking carefully and play slowly at first increasing speed gradually.

## Prelude

## Etude

## The Plectrum Waltz

GUITAR SOLO

CARCASSI-BAY

# THE DOTTED EIGHTH NOTE

A Dotted Eighth-note is equal to

**EXAMPLE:**

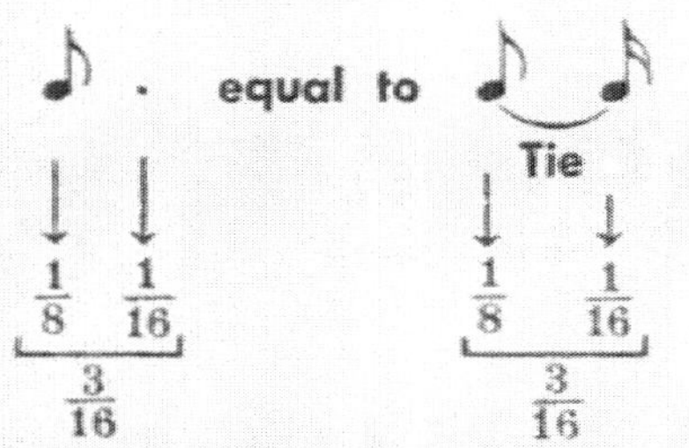


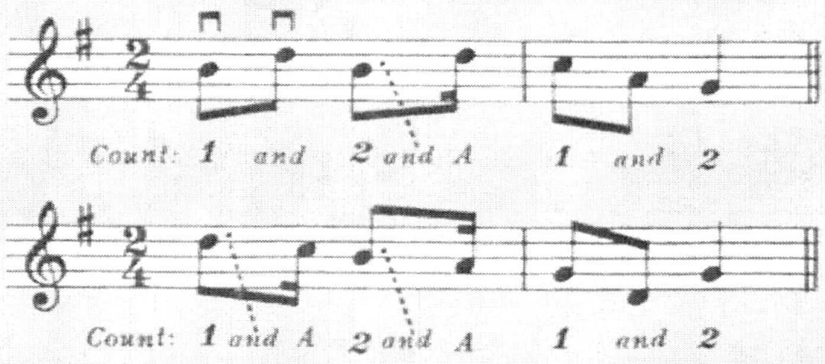


**GUITAR DUET**

## Country Gardens

**ENGLISH FOLK DANCE**

**Arr. by Mel Bay**

Moderato

## Skipping Along

GUITAR SOLO

CARCASSI-BAY

Allegretto

## Coronado

GUITAR SOLO

CARCASSI-BAY

# GUITAR QUARTETS

# CHORALE MELODY

Joseph Castle

**1st GUITAR**

**Allegretto**

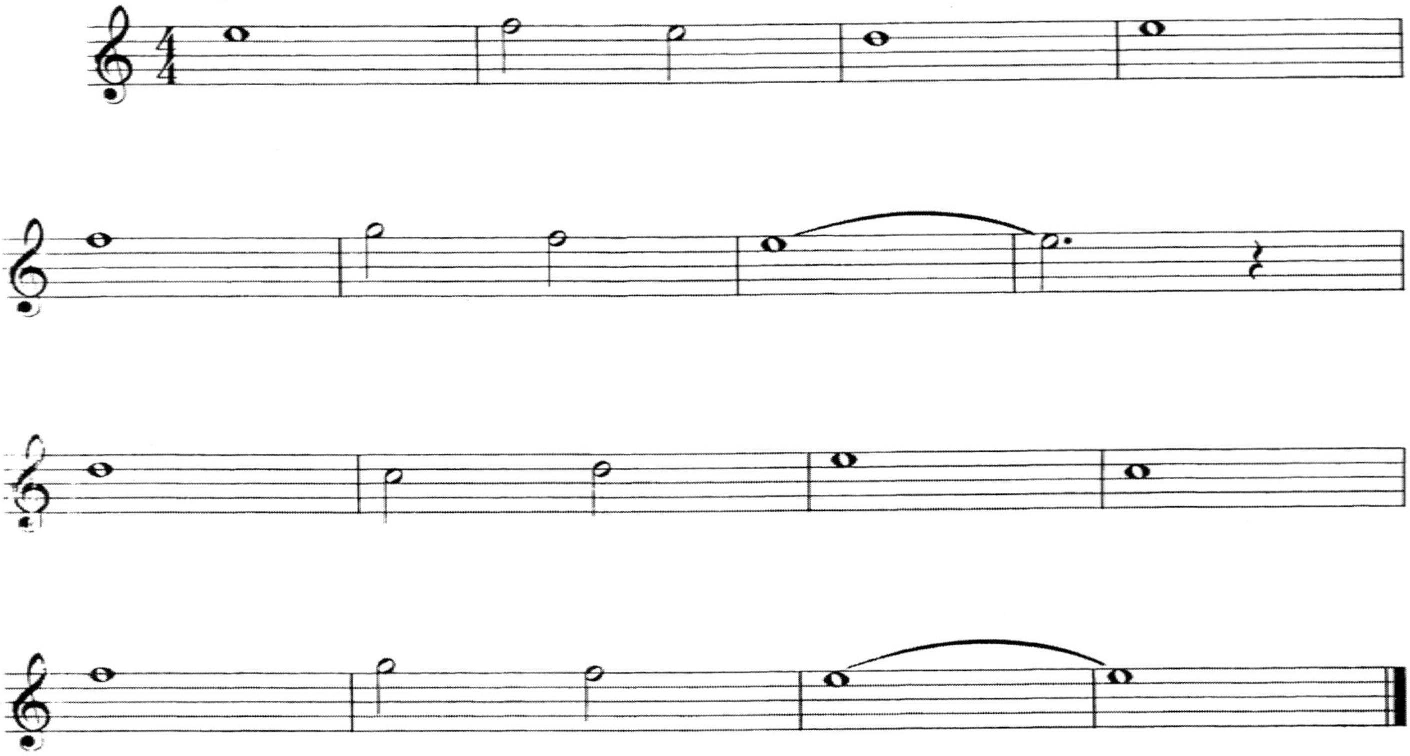

**2nd GUITAR**

**Allegretto**

3rd GUITAR

Allegretto

4th GUITAR

Allegretto

# THEME FROM 9th SYMPHONY

BEETHOVEN

**1st GUITAR**

**Moderato**

**2nd GUITAR**

**Moderato**

## 3rd GUITAR

Moderato

## 4th GUITAR

Moderato

# MELANCHOLY MELODY

PLEYEL

1st GUITAR
Andantino

2nd GUITAR
Andantino

## 3rd GUITAR

Andantino

## 4th GUITAR

Andantino

# MENUET

BACH

**1st GUITAR**

**Allegretto**

**2nd GUITAR**

**Allegretto**

3rd GUITAR

**Allegretto**

4th GUITAR

**Allegretto**

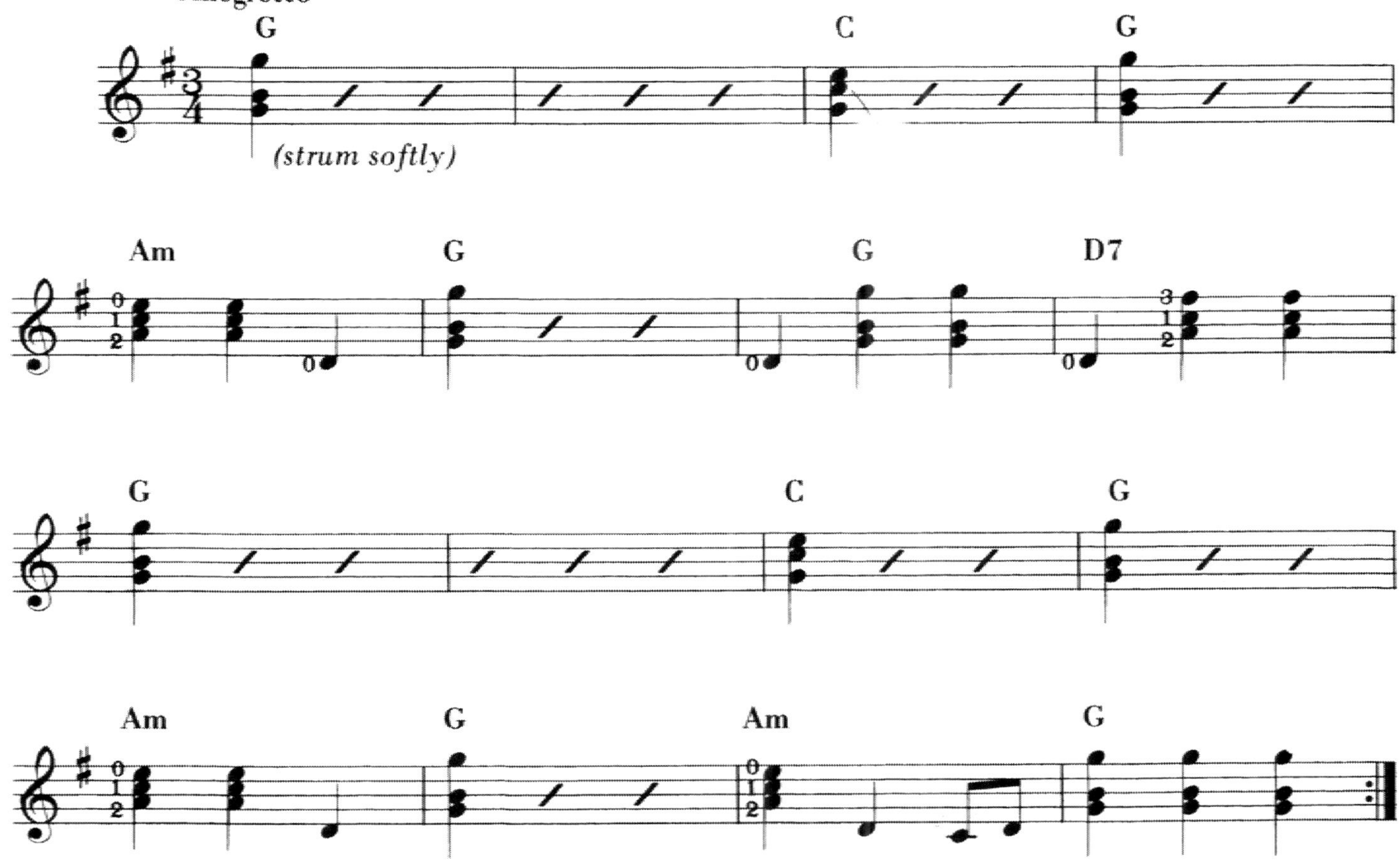

# PRETTY CHORD PROGRESSIONS

**1st GUITAR**

**2nd GUITAR**

### 3rd GUITAR

### 4th GUITAR

# GREENSLEEVES

OLD ENGLISH AIRE

**1st GUITAR**

**Moderato**

**2nd GUITAR**

**Moderato**

## 3rd GUITAR

Moderato

## 4th GUITAR

Moderato

# ADESTE FIDELES

**1st GUITAR**
**Moderato**

**2nd GUITAR**
**Moderato**

3rd GUITAR

Moderato

4th GUITAR

Modearto

# PRELUDE IN E

M. CARCASSI
Op. 59

**1st GUITAR**
**Allegretto**

**2nd GUITAR**
**Allegretto**

### 3rd GUITAR

**Allegretto**

### 4th GUITAR

**Allegretto**

# NOTE READING SOLOS IN VARIOUS STYLES

# Passepied

Moderate Tempo

Handel

# Musetta's Waltz

From "La Boheme"

Moderate, Flowing Tempo

Puccini

# Chorale

Moderately

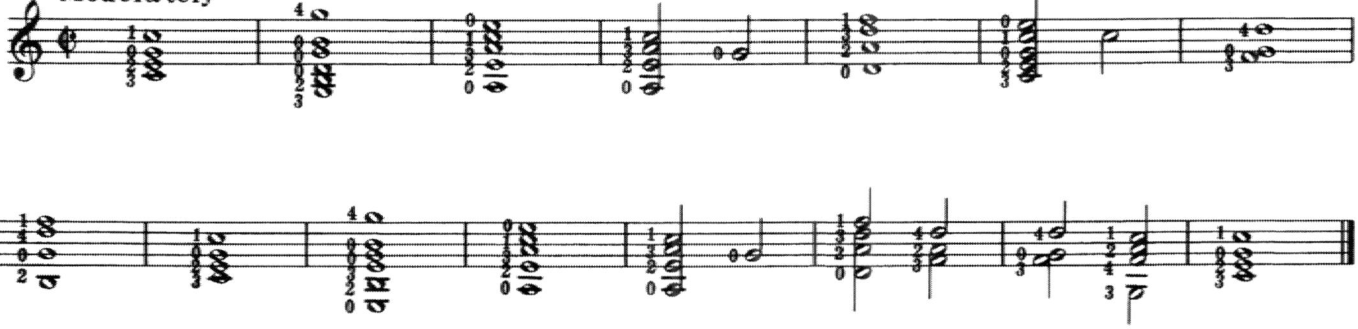

# Andantino

# Melancholy

# Minuet

Slowly

J.S. Bach

# Chorale

Slowly

J. S. Bach

# Puppet Waltz

Moderate Tempo

Bill Bay

# Driftin'

Slow

Bill Bay

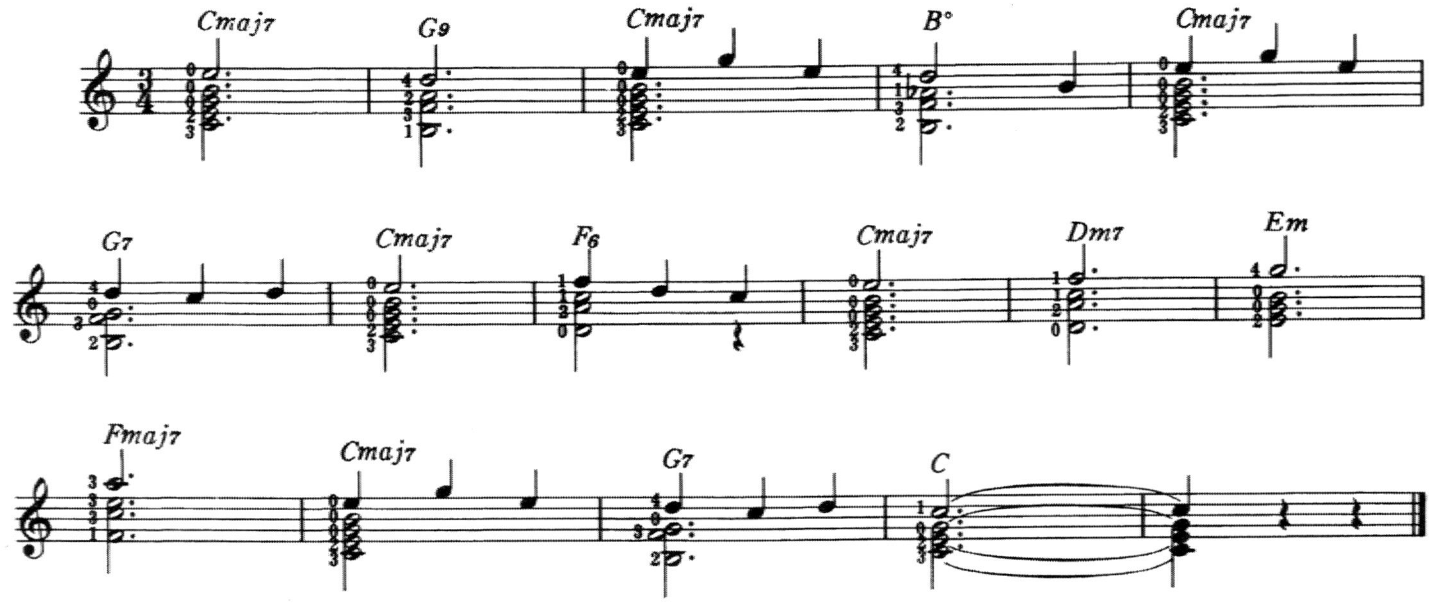


# Bossa Nova Intro (in key of C)

(Play Chords Pictured)

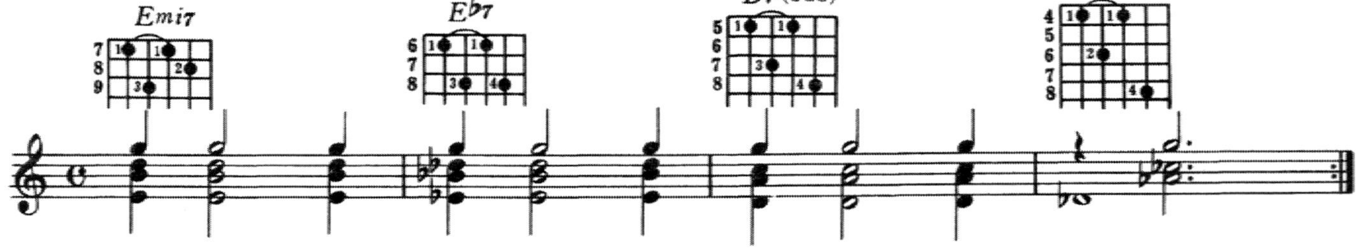

# Flamenco Prelude

**Slow Ad lib Tempo**

**Bill Bay**

# Caliente

**Moderately**

**Bill Bay**

# Easy Feelin'

**Bill Bay**

Easy Feeling

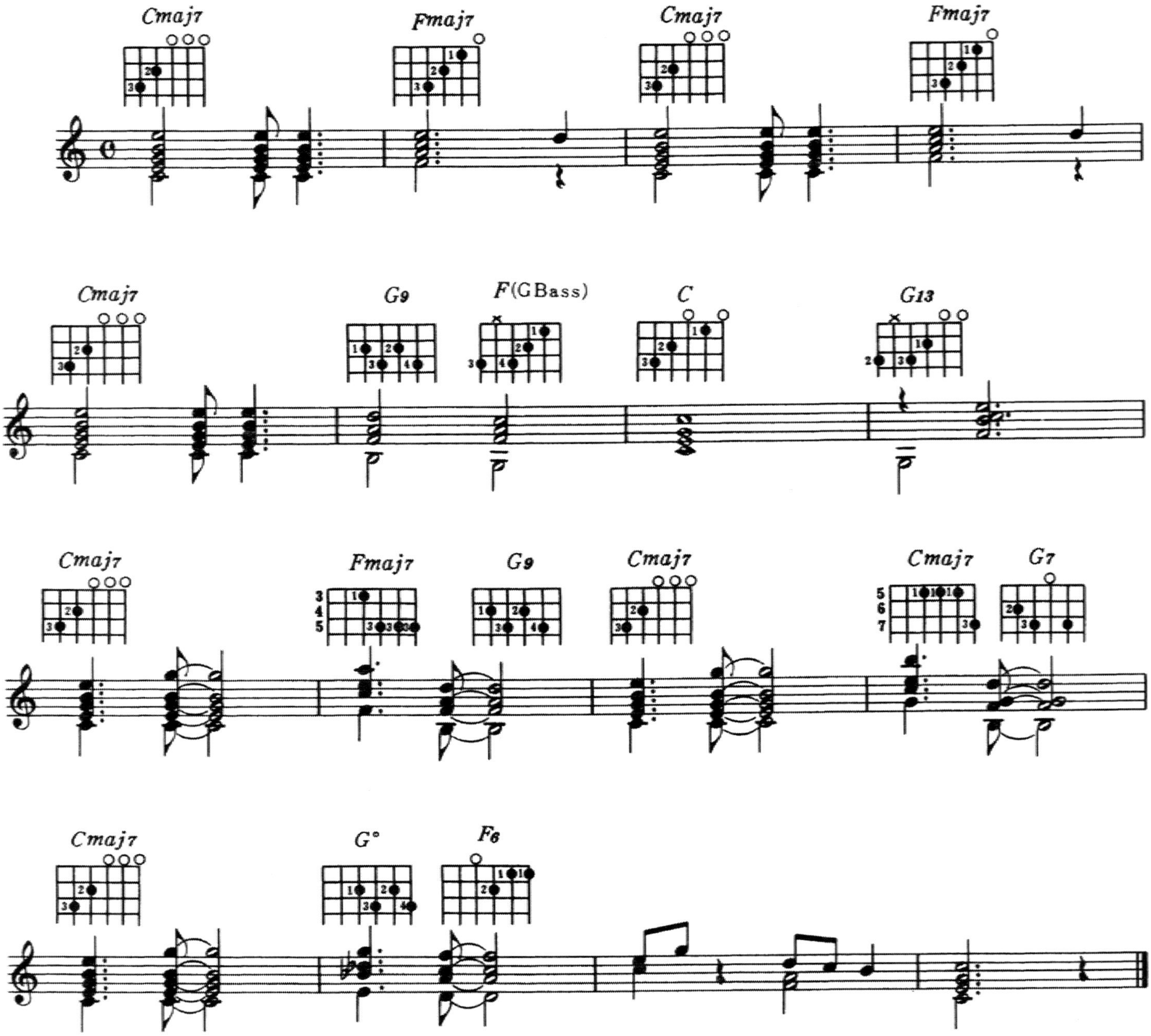


# Mel's Ending

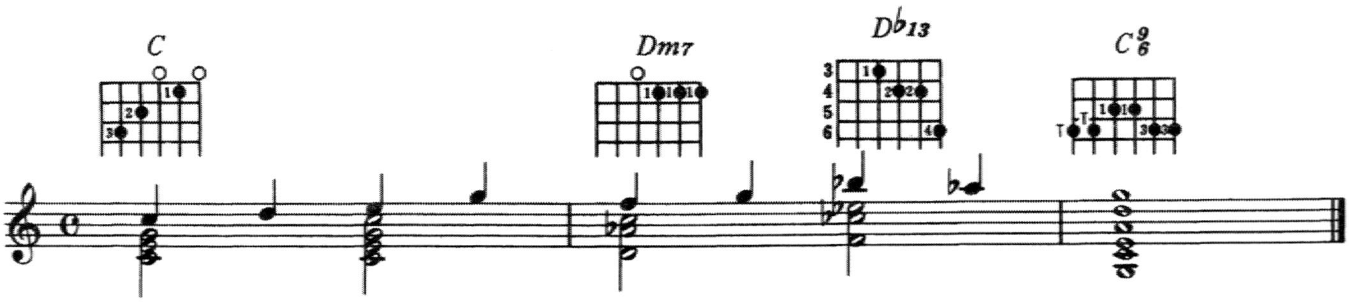

# Interlude

**Slow** **Bill Bay**

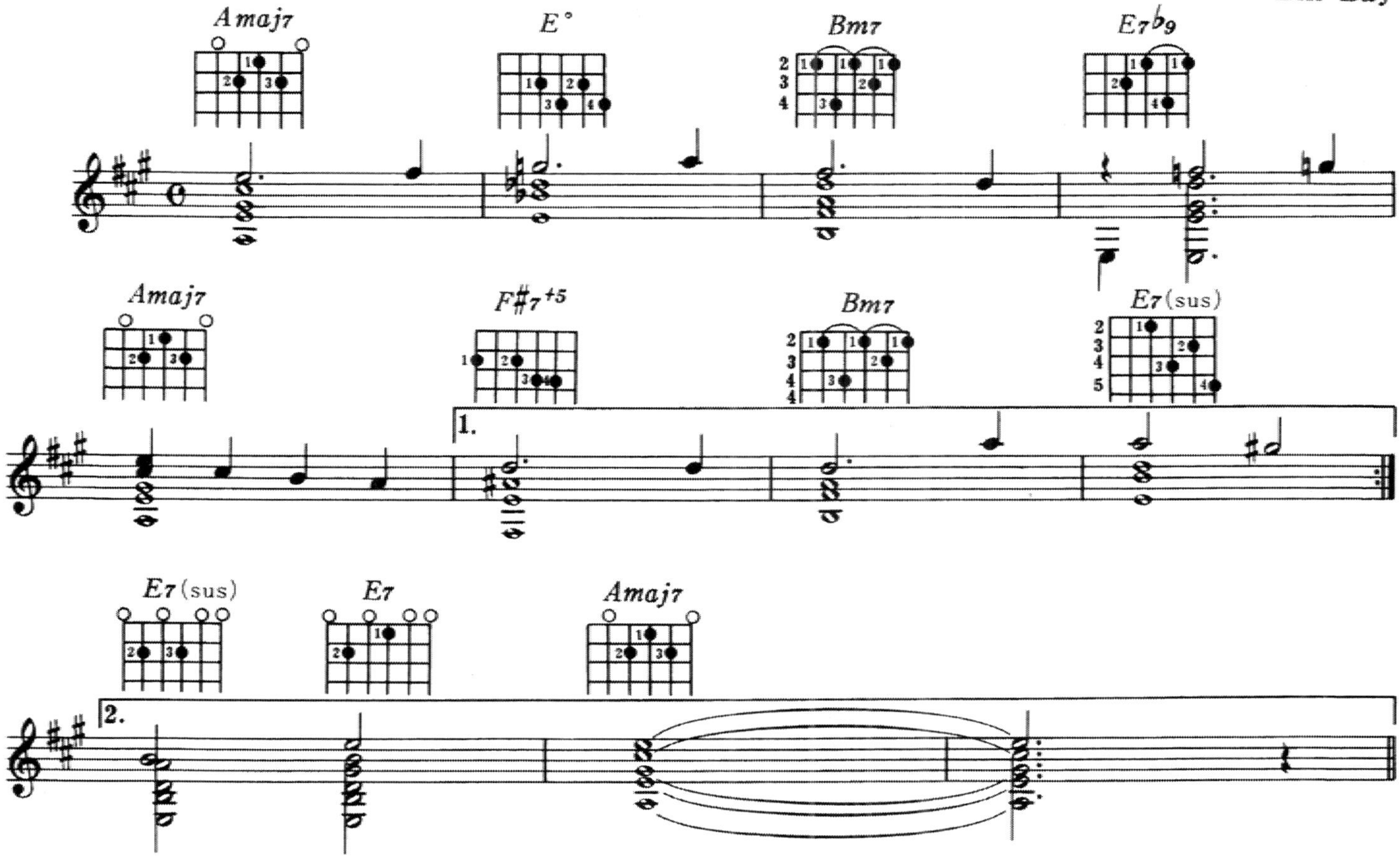


# Images

**Very Slow** **Bill Bay**

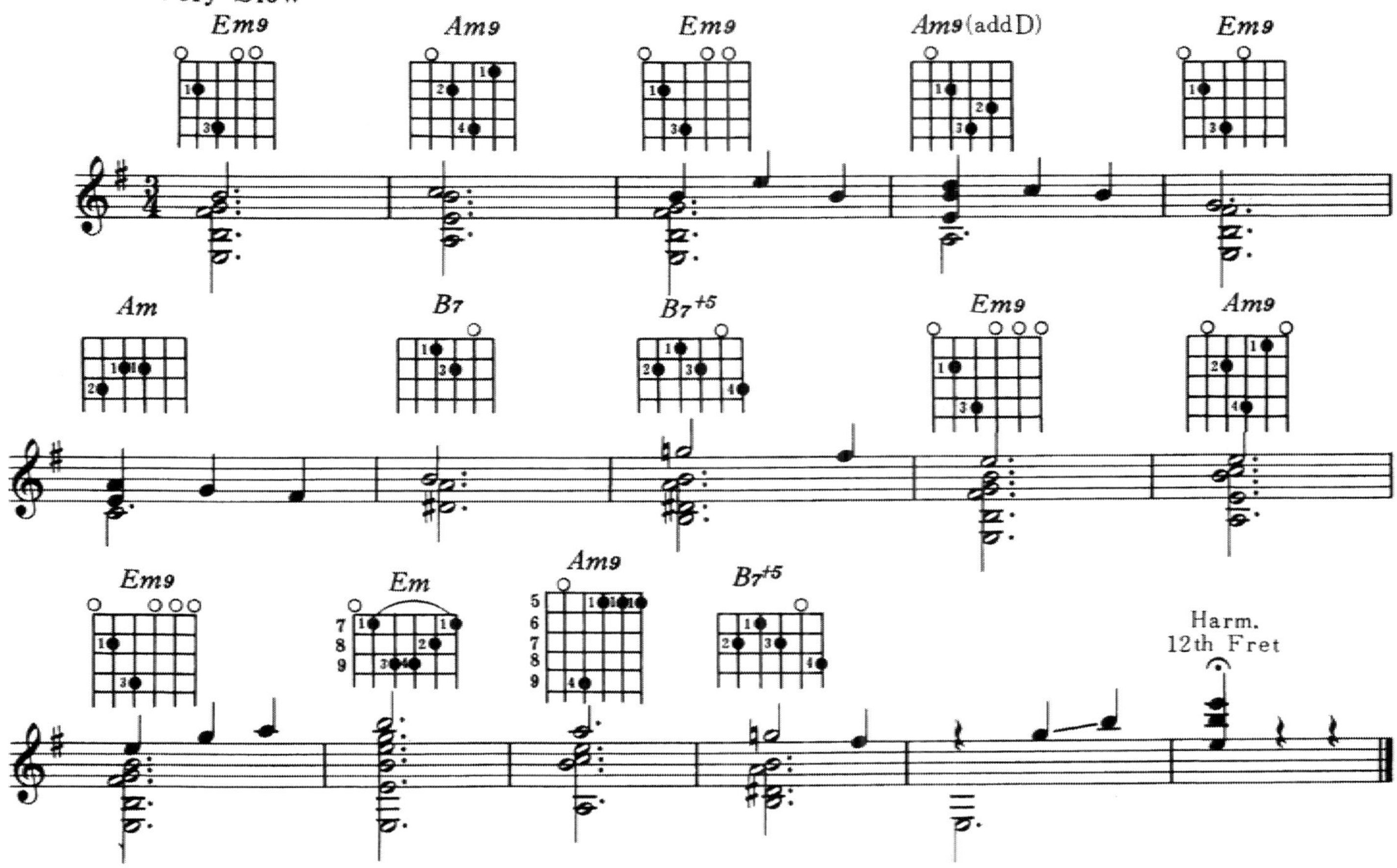

# *Liebestraüme*

*Arr. by Ray Bell*

FRANZ LISZT

**Slowly**

# All Through the Night

*Arr. by Ray Bell*

DAVID OWEN

# *Theme from Symphony No. 1*

*Arr. by Ray Bell*

JOHANNES BRAHMS

**Moderato**

# Evening Chimes

*Arr. by Ray Bell*

**Moderately**

# Moonlight Sonata

*Arr. by Ray Bell*

L. Van BEETHOVEN

Slowly

# Come With Me, My Giselle

**Slowly**

Adam De la Halle (1230-1287)

# Wild Horsemen

(Plectrum Study)

**Lively Tempo**

# America

# Wee Bryn

Bill Bay

Slowly

# Lakewood Meadows

Bill Bay

# Meditation

Bill Bay

# MELODY CHORD SOLO PLAYING

# THE GUITAR FINGERBOARD

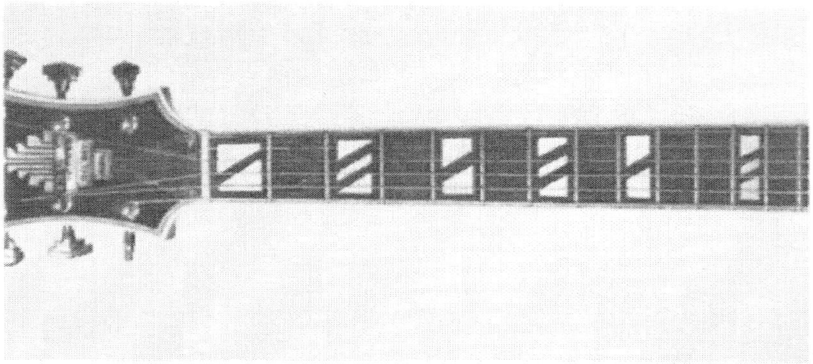

THE DIAGRAM OF THE FINGERBOARD

READING UPWARD THE STRINGS WILL BE NUMBERED: ⑥ ⑤ ④ ③ ② ①

⑥ – Largest string. ① – Smallest string.

The encircled numbers 6 5 4 3 2 1 will be the numbers of the STRINGS.

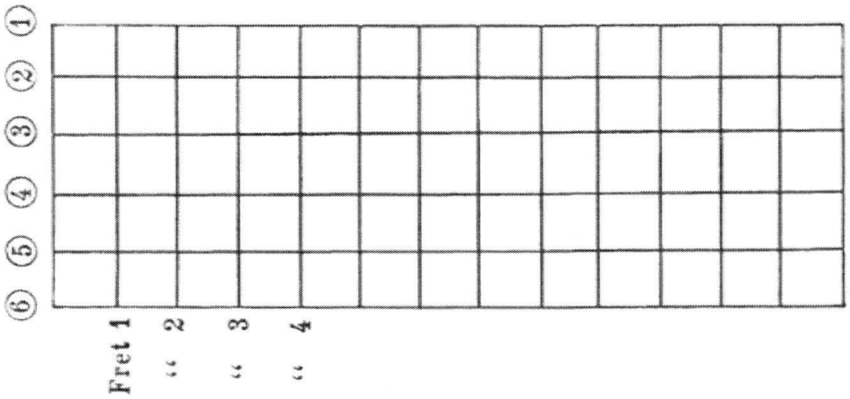


The horizontal lines are the strings. The vertical lines are the frets.

THE NOTES ON THE GUITAR AN OCTAVE HIGHER (8va)

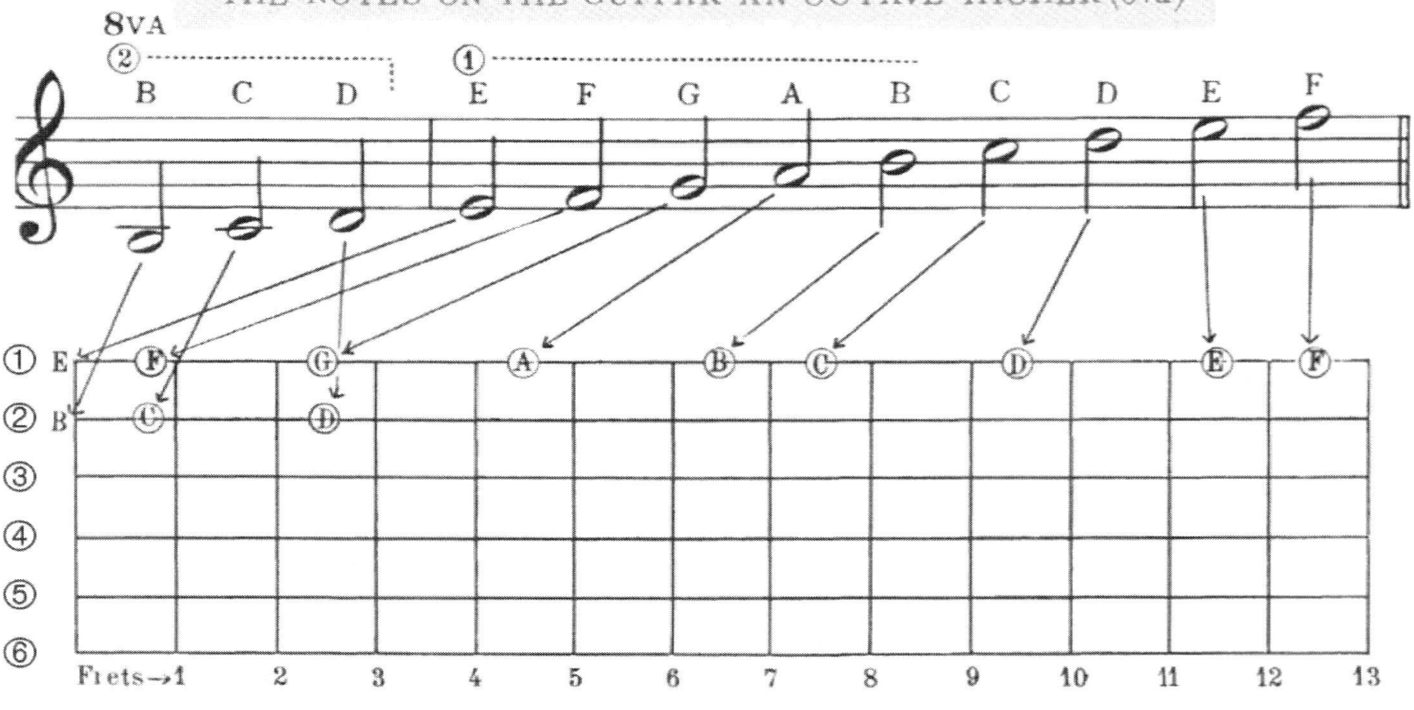

# THE TABLATURE

The horizontal lines are the GUITAR STRINGS.
The number on each STRING indicates FRET LOCATION.
The number in parenthesis ( ) indicates LEFT HAND FINGER.
The encircled number ◯ at the head of the Tablature indicates the number of the string,
ⓧ = String not played.

## EXAMPLE

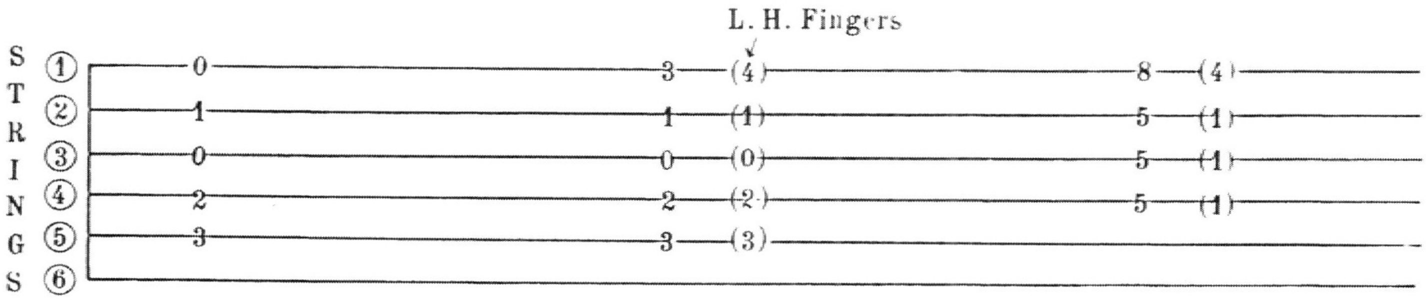


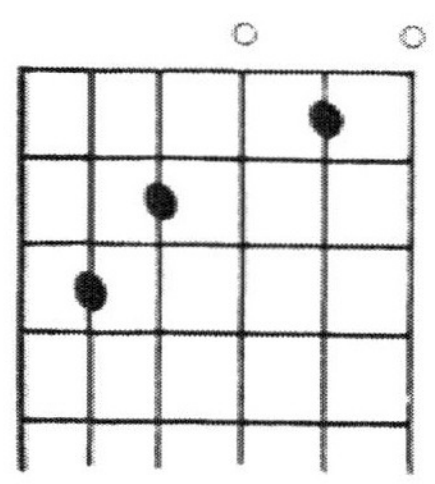

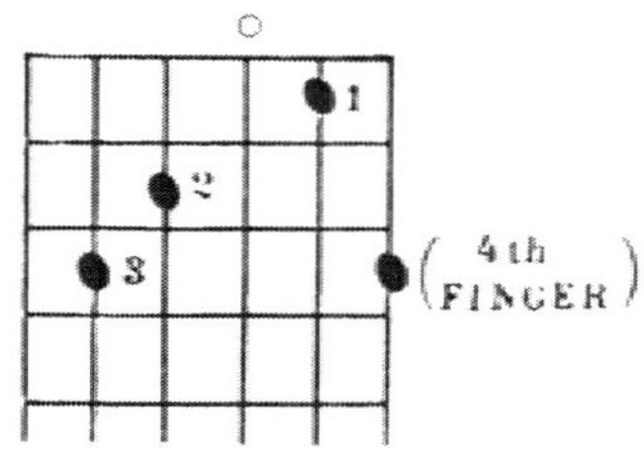


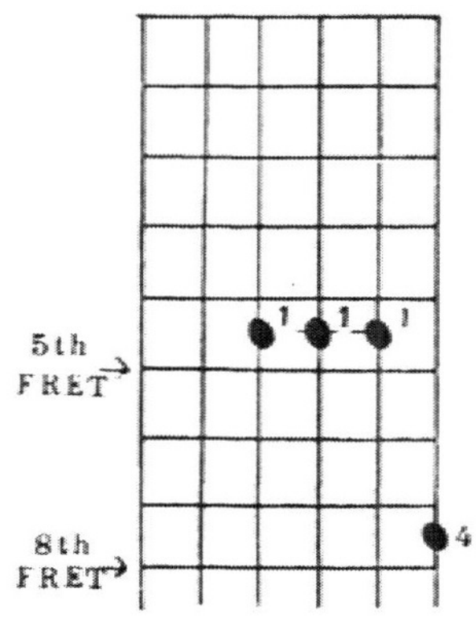


The musical notation will be as in the voice or melody line of the popular song sheets.

PLAY 8VA

EXAMPLE

Play this line:

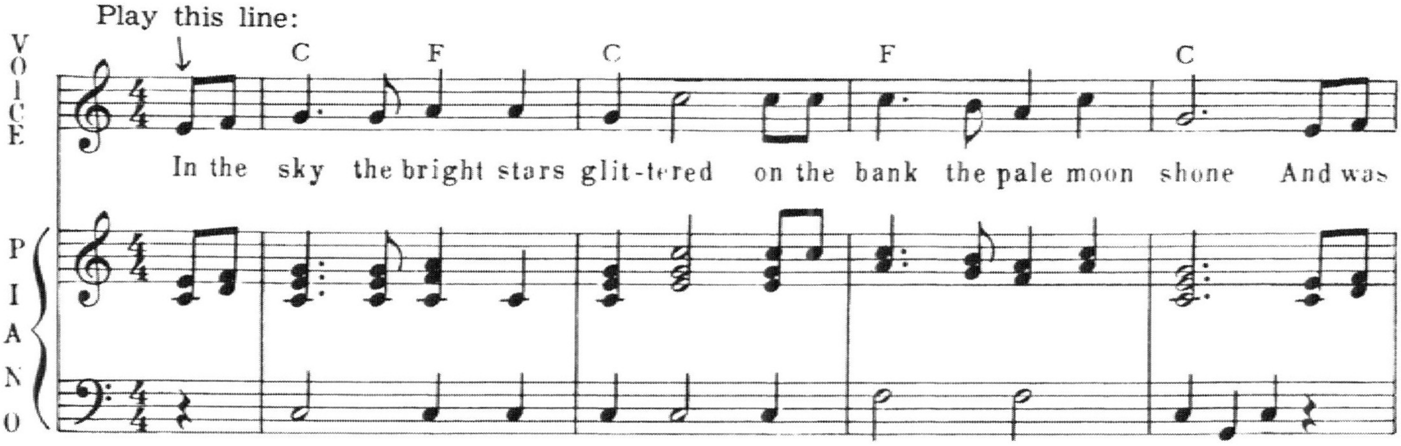


REMEMBER—All Music to be Played 8va
(One Octave Higher than written)

# THE MAJOR CHORD FORMS

Play each form Chromatically up and down the fingerboard until mastered.

## FORM I

Practice from First to the Tenth Frets.

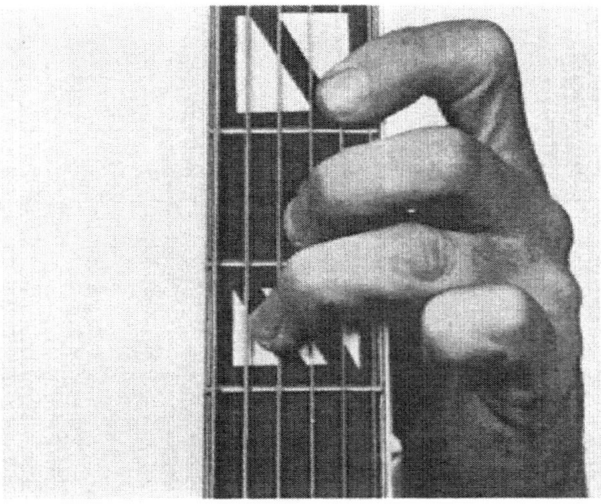

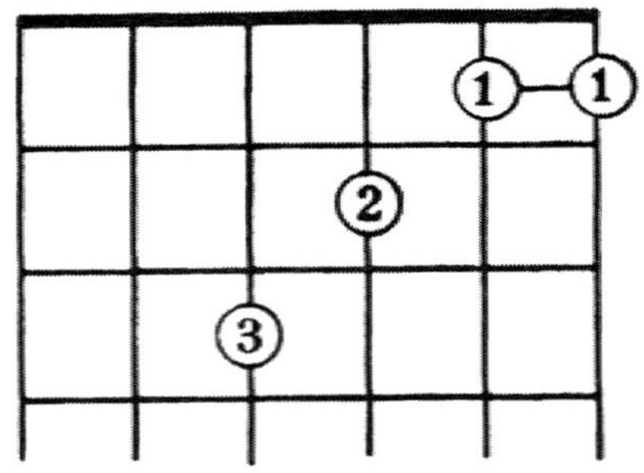


## FORM III

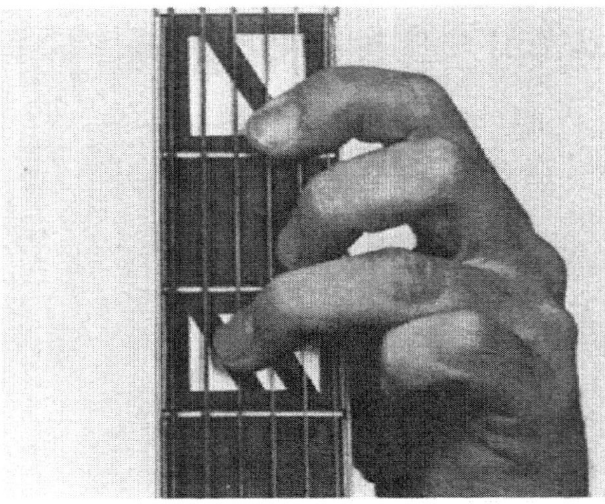

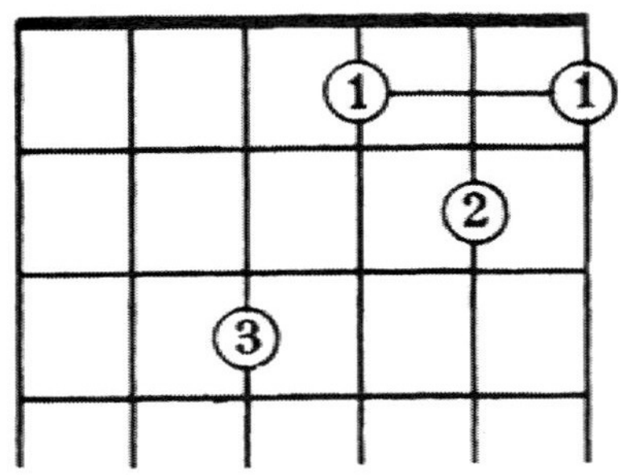


## FORM V

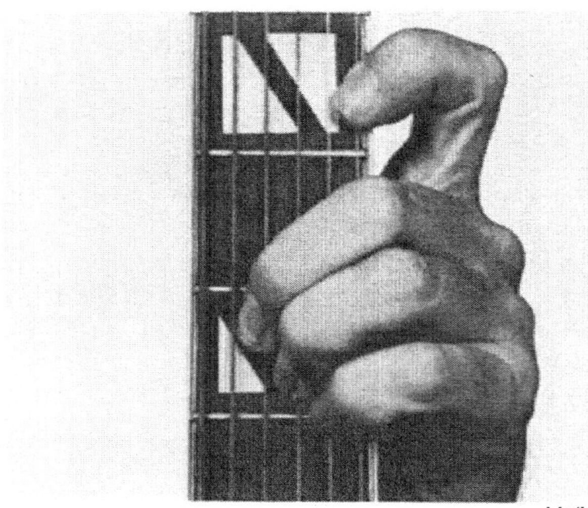

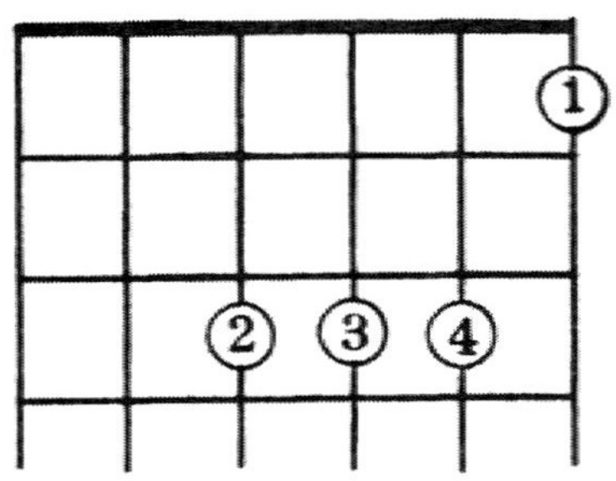

# THE SEVENTH CHORD FORMS

Symbol for Seventh Chord (7)

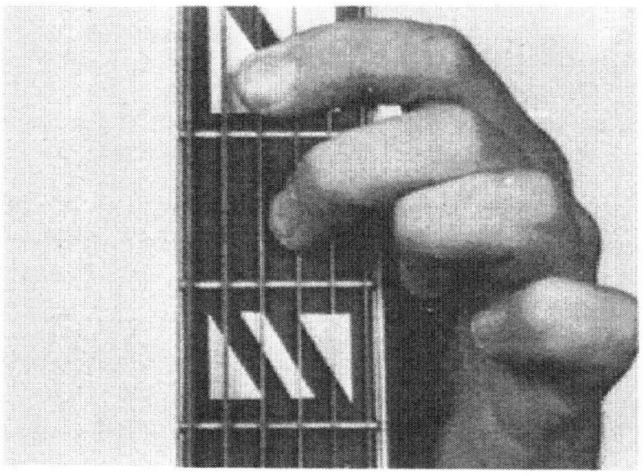

## FORM I7

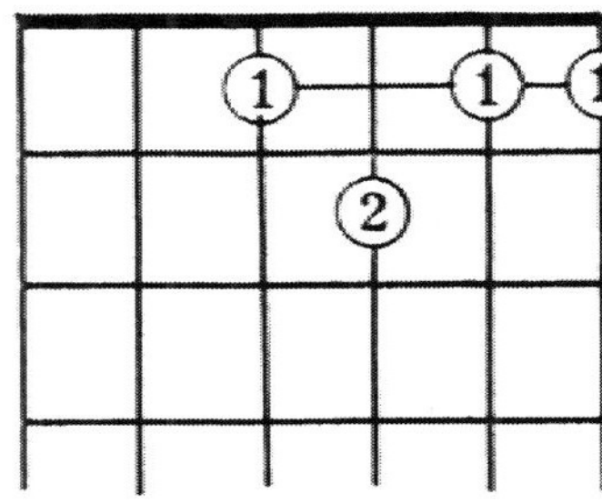


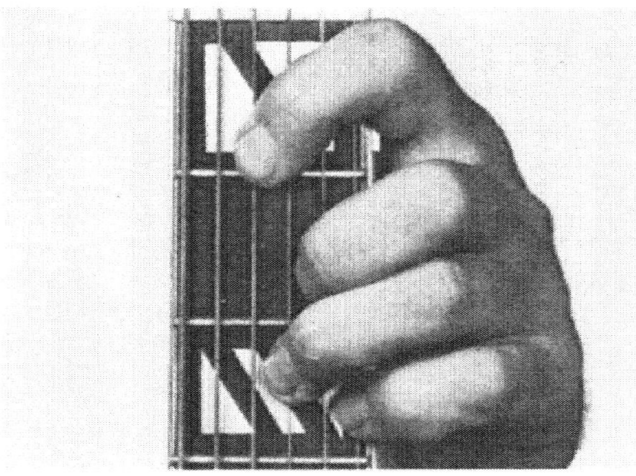

## FORM III7

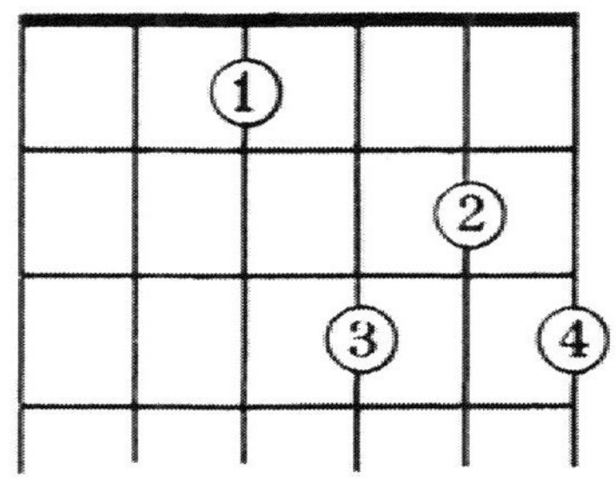


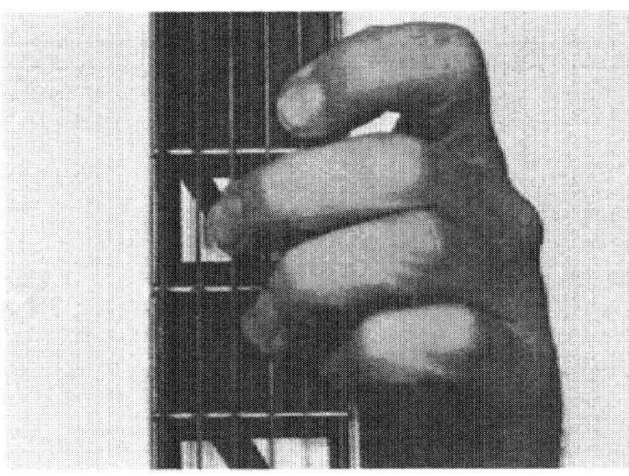

## FORM V7

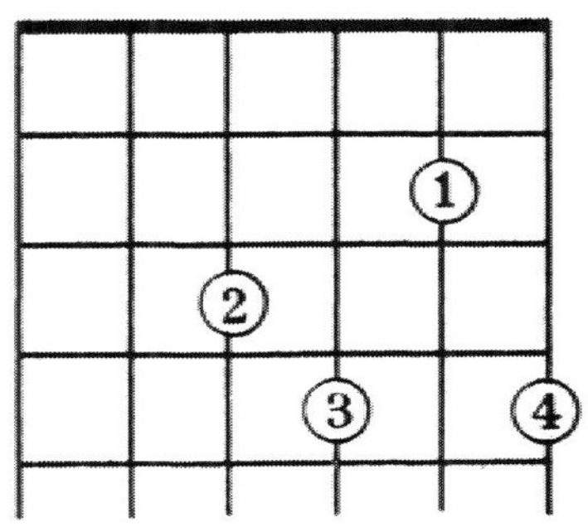


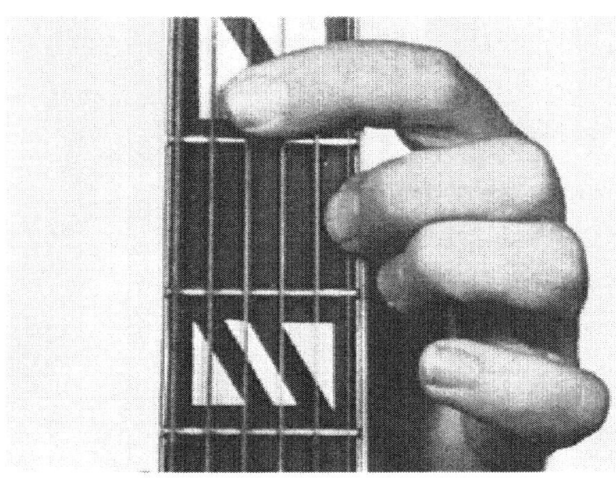

## FORM VII7

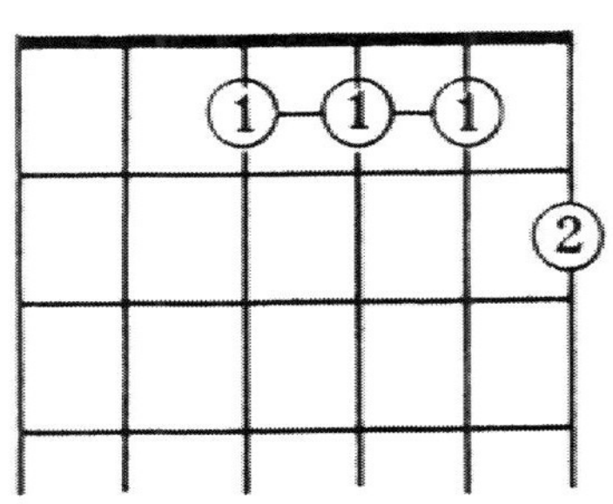

## OPTIONAL FORMS

Sometimes a chord form will be difficult to reach thus causing a loss of tempo in melody chord playing. This may be facilitated by employing an OPTIONAL FORM.

Our first optional major chord form is optional form I. (Symbol: op. I).

OP.–I

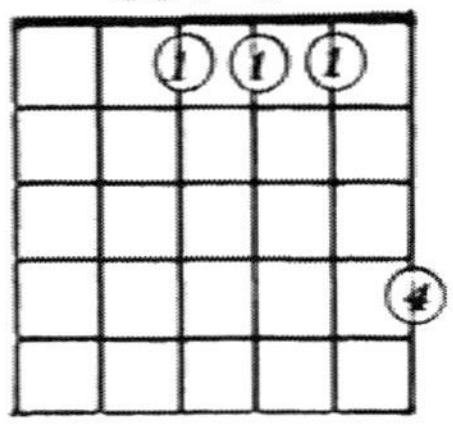

TABLATURE

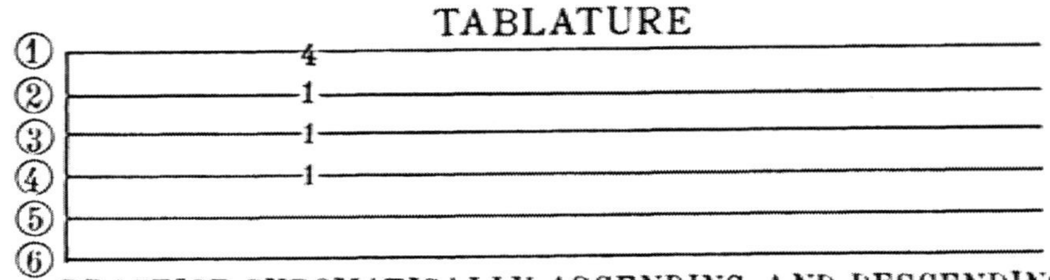


PRACTICE CHROMATICALLY ASCENDING AND DESCENDING

Our next optional form is optional form V. (Symbol: op. V).
This form is best made by holding form III and lowering the 4th finger on the 1st string as indicated.

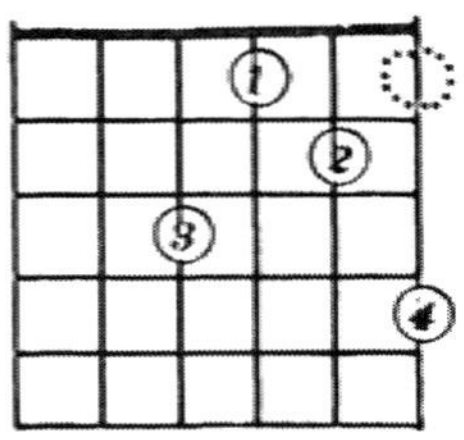

TABLATURE

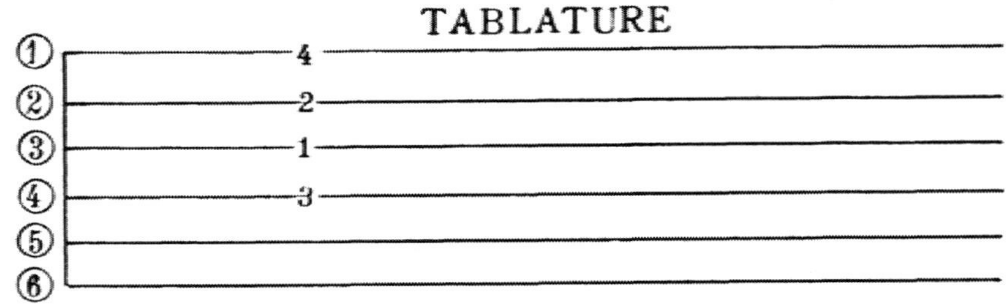


### THE C CHORDS

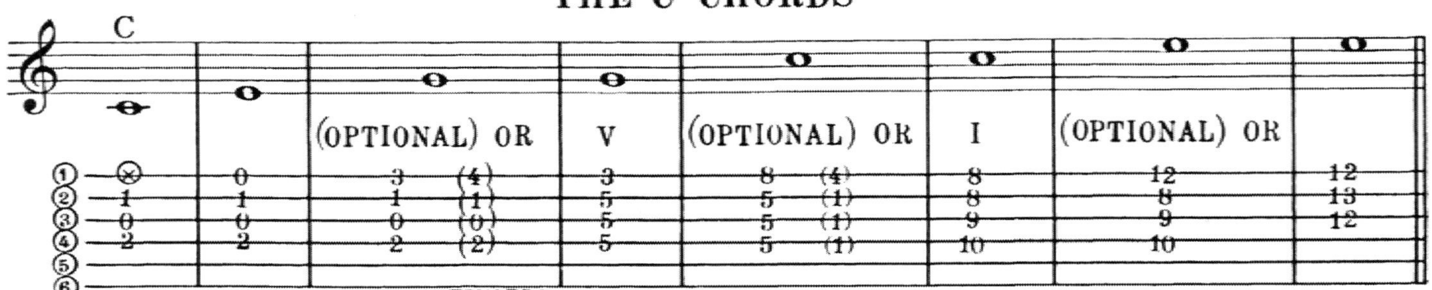


FINGERS

⊗=String not played. Note also that strings ⑤ and ⑥ are not used at this time.

### THE F CHORDS

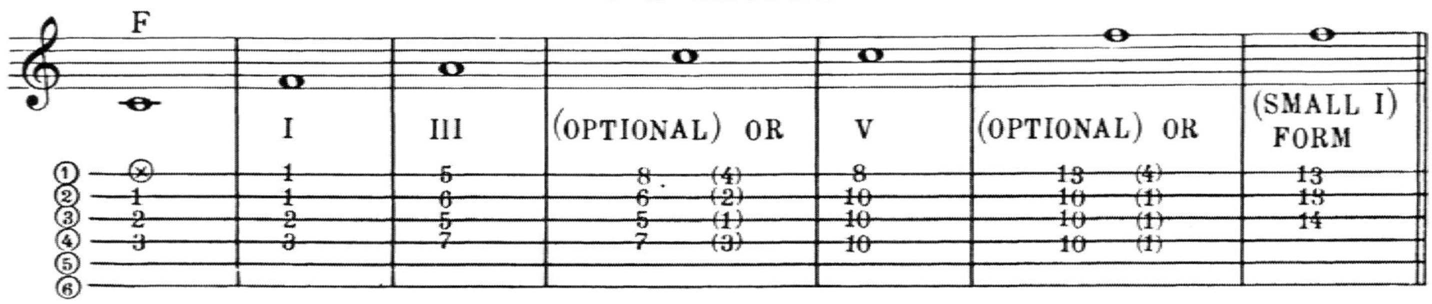


### THE G7 CHORDS

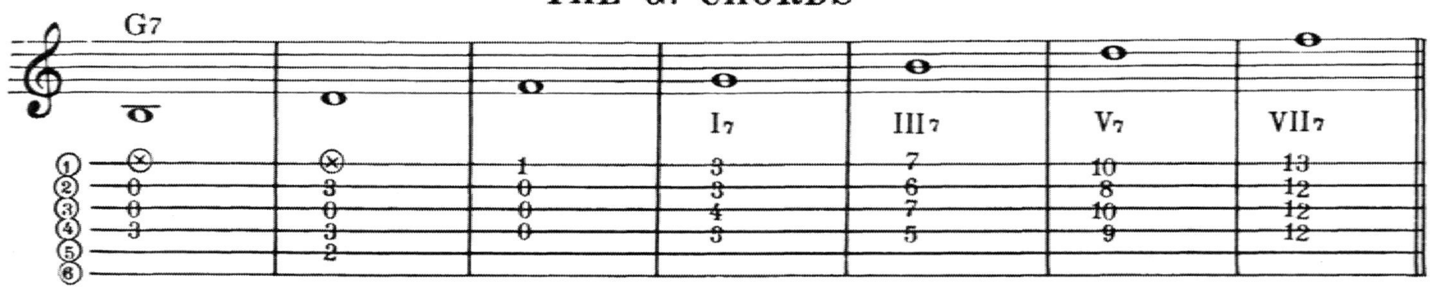

PRACTICE THE FOLLOWING CHORD STUDIES IN THIS MANNER:

1– One strum per chord. Strum slowly in a harplike fashion. (⁞ = Harplike).

2– Strum each chord four times on the whole-notes and two strums for each half-note.

𝅝 = //// 𝅗𝅥 = // A quarter note will receive one strum. ♩ = /

3– Pick the melody note as a single note followed by three strums for the whole-notes and one single note followed by one strum for each half-note.

X = single note 𝅝 = X /// 𝅗𝅥 = X /

## CHORD STUDY IN THE KEY OF C

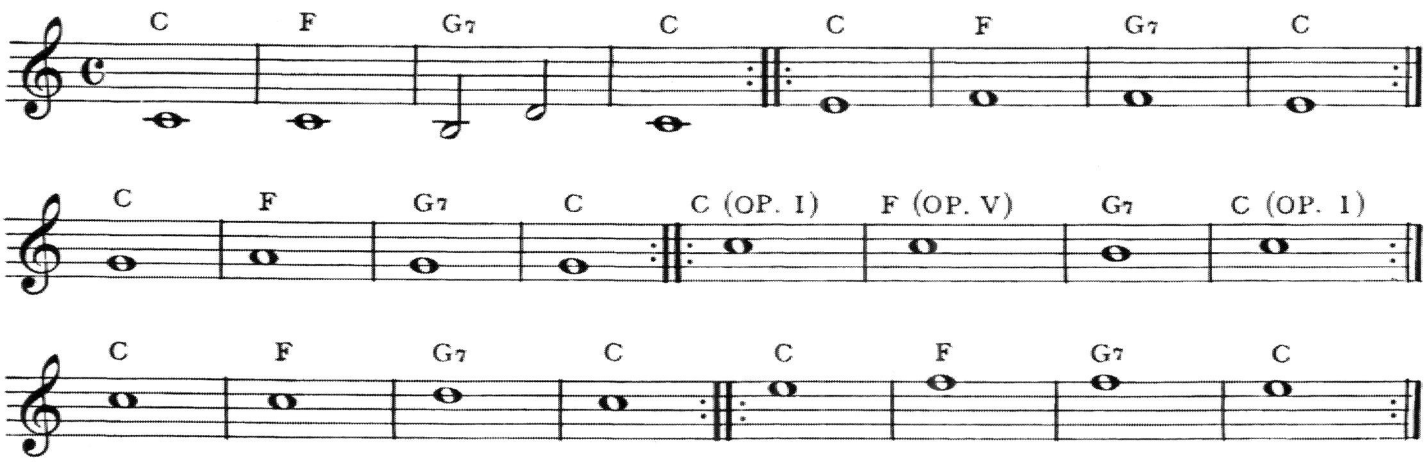


## THE C SCALE HARMONIZED

## CHORD SONG IN C

(x=Single note)

The chords in the key of C are: C, F and G7. This is the family of chords in the key of C.

## Long, Long Ago

## On Top Of Old Smokey

Play the dotted half-notes harplike in the first chorus and the second chorus in this manner (x=//). A single note followed by two chord strokes.

## THE NOTES ON THE THIRD STRING (G)

(IN 8va NOTATION)

In most melodies, the notes on the third string will be played as single notes. (X)

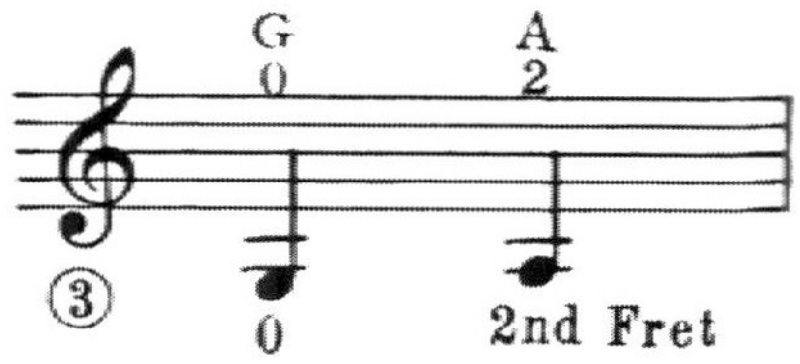


The two notes on the 3d string:

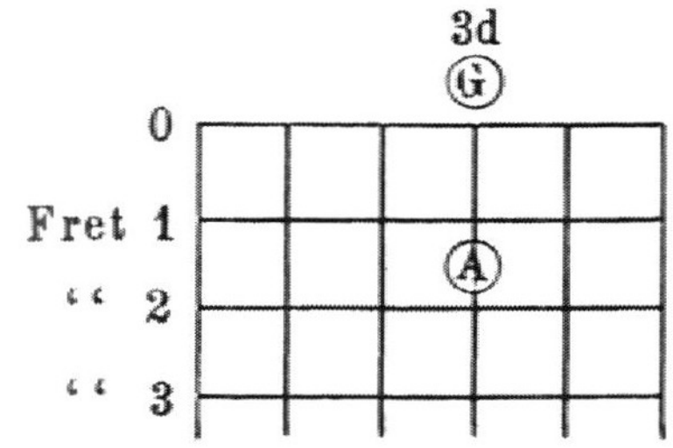


# Down In The Valley

A review of the high and low position chords

# The Quilting Party

SEEING NELLIE HOME

# THE CHORDAL TONES

Chordal tones belong to the structure of the chord.

The Major chord construction consists of the root, third and fifth notes of the Major Scale. (1st, 3rd and 5th) This explains the naming of the chord forms Form I, Form III and Form V. The TOPNOTE or MELODY NOTE will be as named in the form number.

example:

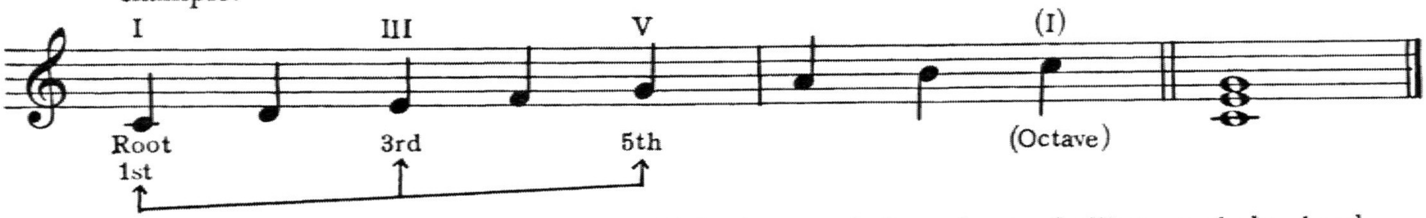


Theoretical construction and concept will be bypassed. In order to facilitate melody chord playing, only basic theory will be employed. A complete course in theory and harmony is recommended as a supplement to this book or as a follow up for good musicianship.

# THE NON CHORDAL TONES

A Non-Chordal tone is a tone not belonging to the chord.
As explained above, the C chord contains the following notes: C-E-G.
All other notes in the C scale are Non-Chordal. (Not a part of the chord)

In the example note that the chordal tones are designated I, III and V. The Non-Chordal tones will be in parenthesis.

The tones Non-Chordal to the C chord are D, F, A and B.

Harmonizing a Non-Chordal tone will be done in this manner:

1. Place the Major form nearest to the Non-Chordal tone.
2. Substitute the top-note with the Non-Chordal tone leaving the remaining portion of the chord undisturbed. In other words, the chordal top-note will be replaced by the Non-Chordal top-note.

HARMONIZING THE NON-CHORDAL TONES WITH THE C CHORD

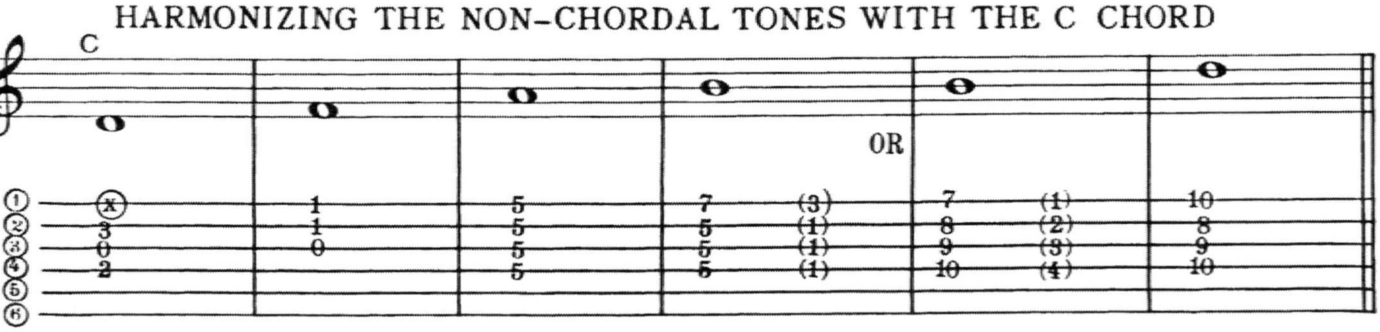


HARMONIZING THE C SCALE WITH THE C CHORD

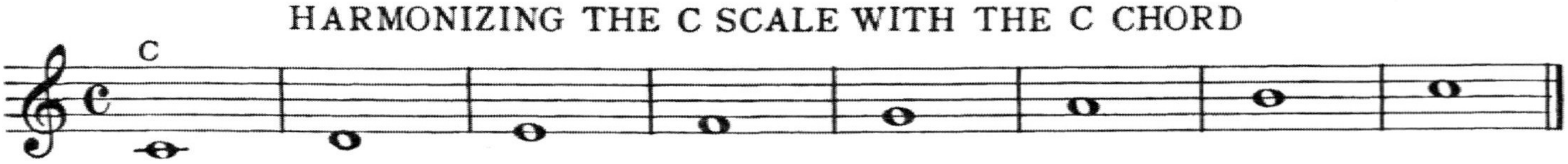

## HARMONIZING THE NON-CHORDAL TONES WITH THE F CHORD

THE CHORDAL TONES OF THE F CHORD ARE: F–A–C

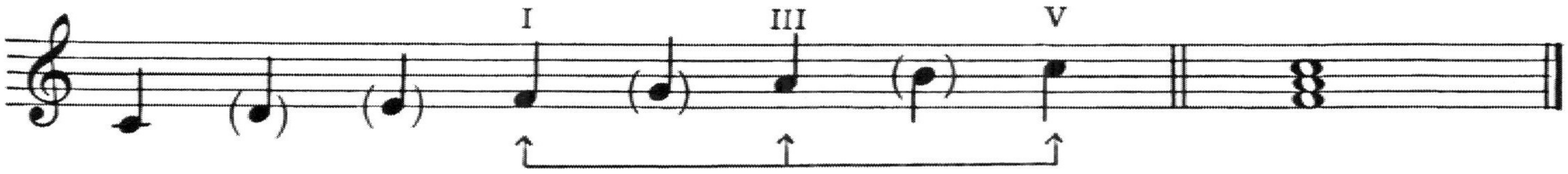


THE NON-CHORDAL TONES ARE: G–B–D–F

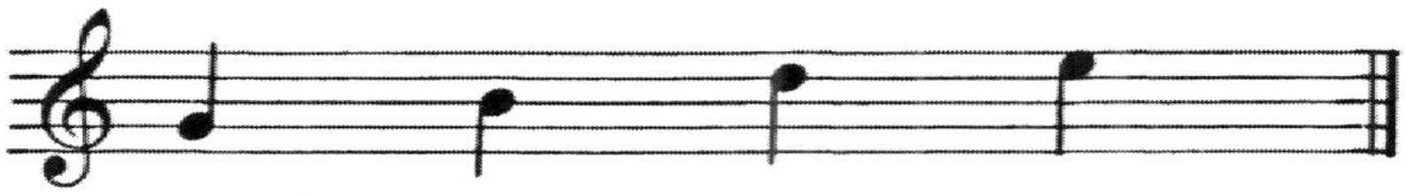

THE NON-CHORDAL TONES HARMONIZED WITH THE F CHORD

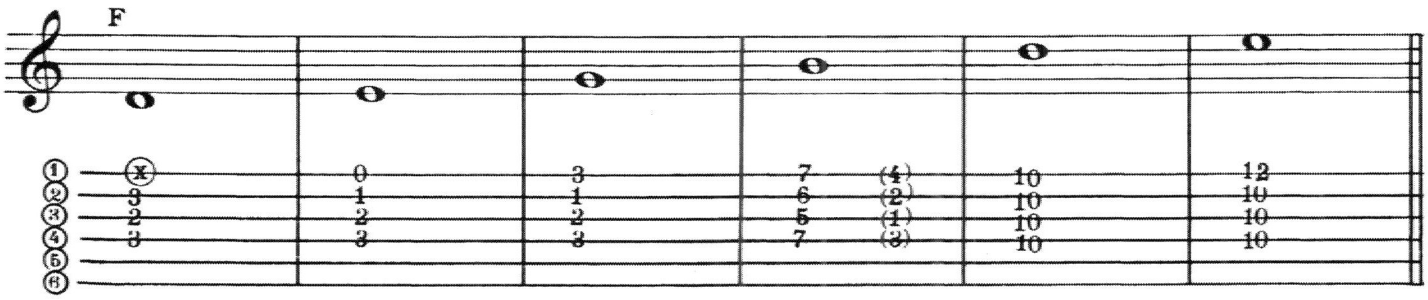


## HARMONIZING THE NON-CHORDAL TONES WITH THE G7 CHORD

THE CHORDAL TONES OF THE G7 CHORD ARE: G–B–D–F

(Key of C)

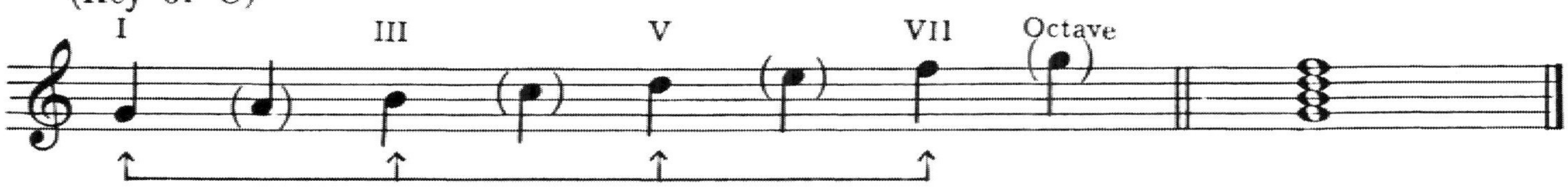


THE NON-CHORDAL TONES ARE: A–C–E

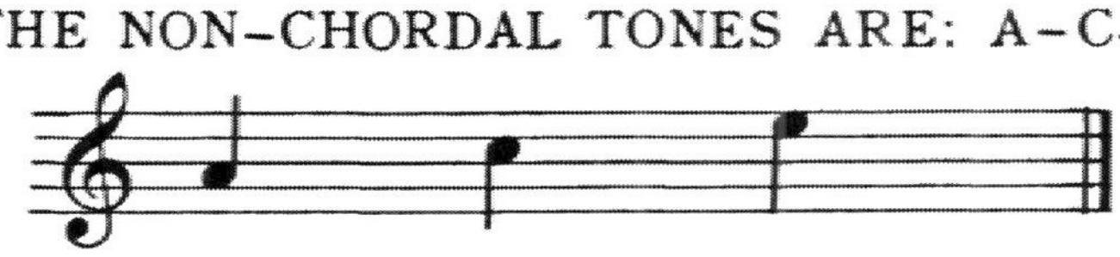

THE NON-CHORDAL TONES HARMONIZED WITH THE G7 CHORD

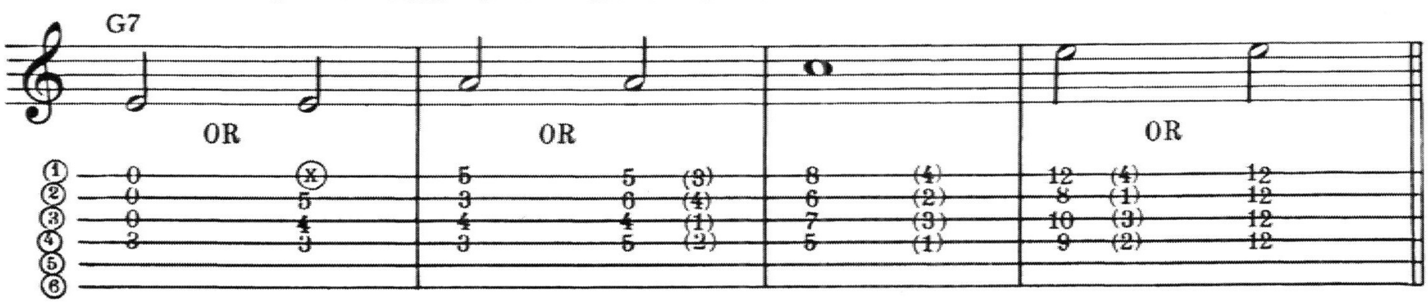

## A STUDY HARMONIZING CHORDAL AND NON-CHORDAL TONES

The non-chordal tones will be indicated in this manner (   ).

## ANOTHER STUDY IN HARMONIZING CHORDAL AND NON-CHORDAL TONES

# THE MINOR CHORD FORMS

Symbol for Minor (M)

## MINOR FORM IM

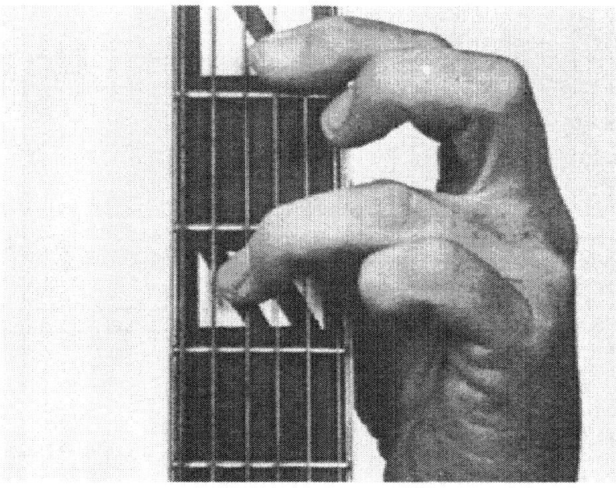

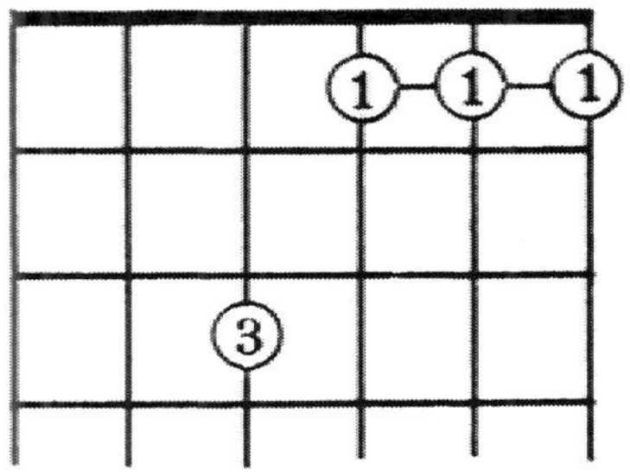


## MINOR FORM IIIM

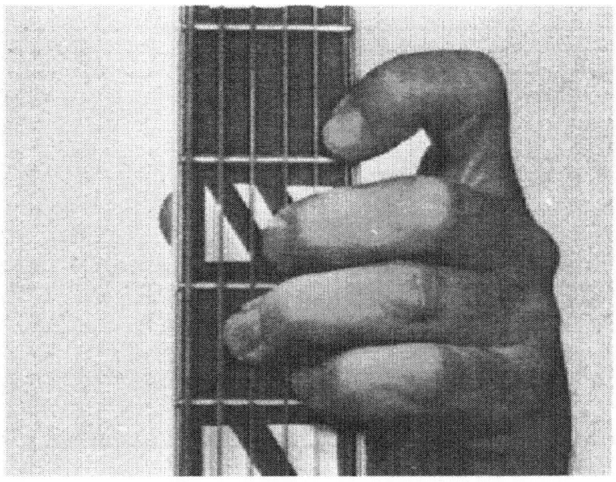

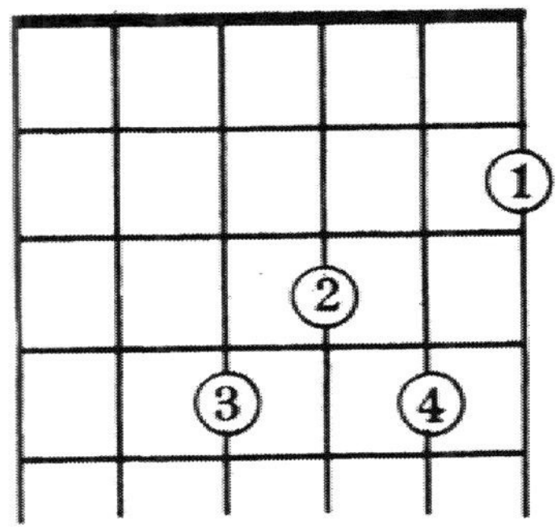


## MINOR FORM VM

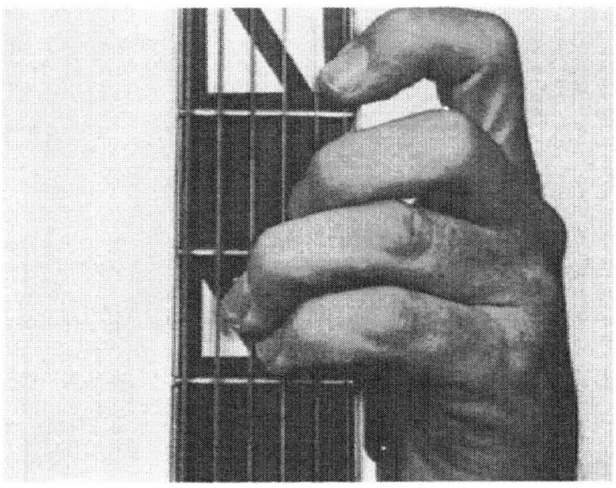

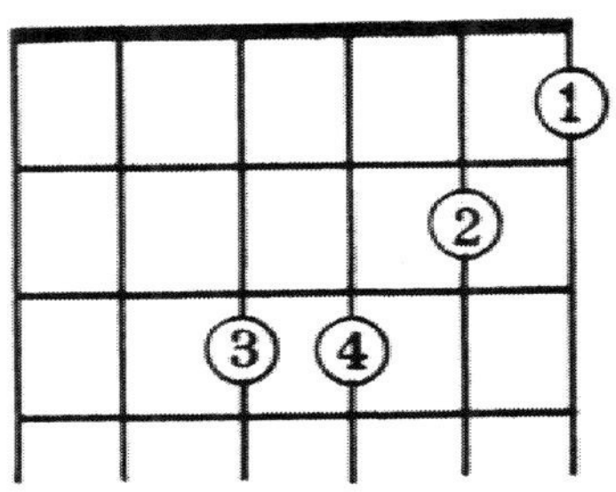

# THE MELODY CHORDS IN THE KEY OF A MINOR

(RELATIVE TO THE KEY OF C MAJOR)

## THE A MINOR CHORDS

SYMBOL: Am
CHORD SPELLING: A-C-E

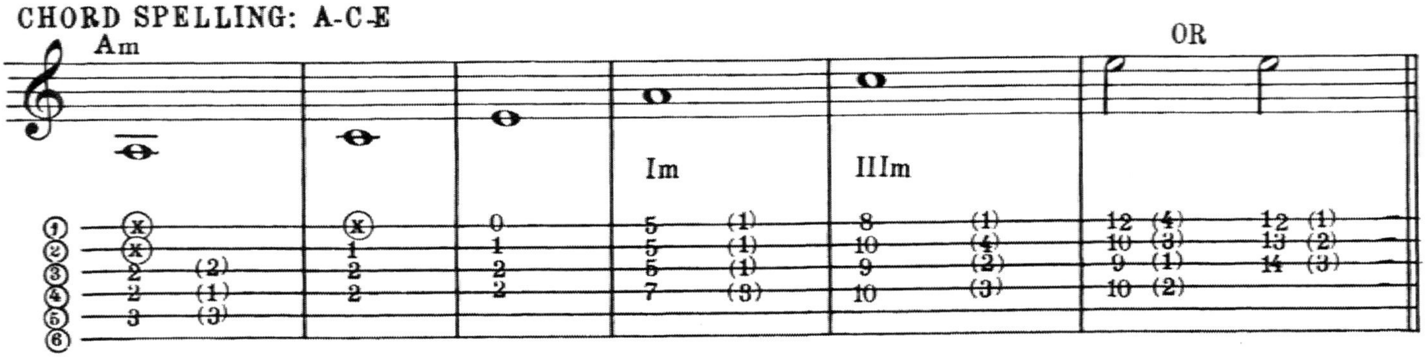


## THE D MINOR CHORDS

SYMBOL: Dm
CHORD SPELLING: D-F-A

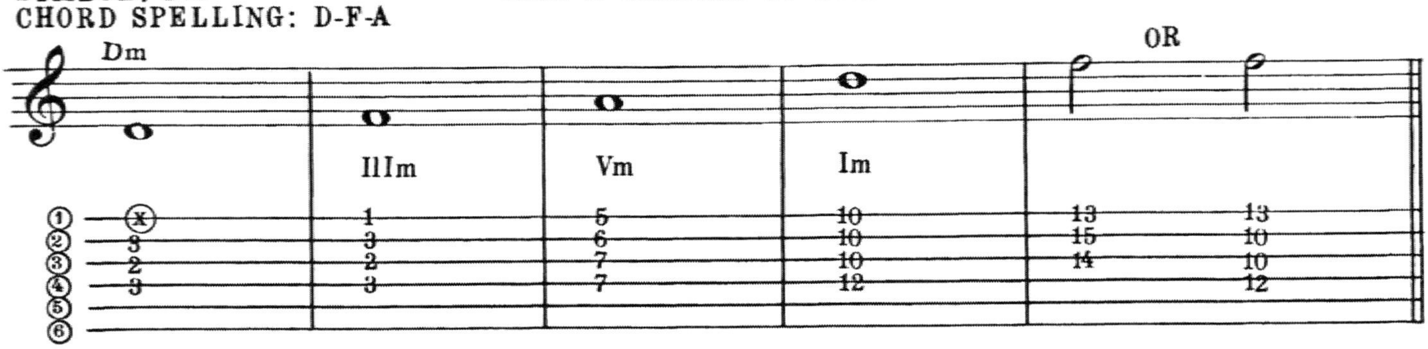


## THE E7 CHORDS

SYMBOL: E7
CHORD SPELLING: E-G♯-B-D

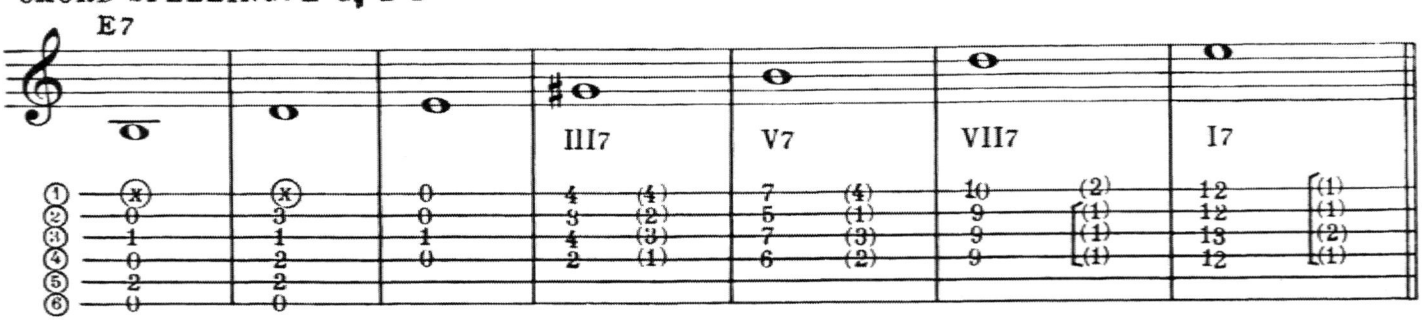


## CHORD STUDY IN A MINOR

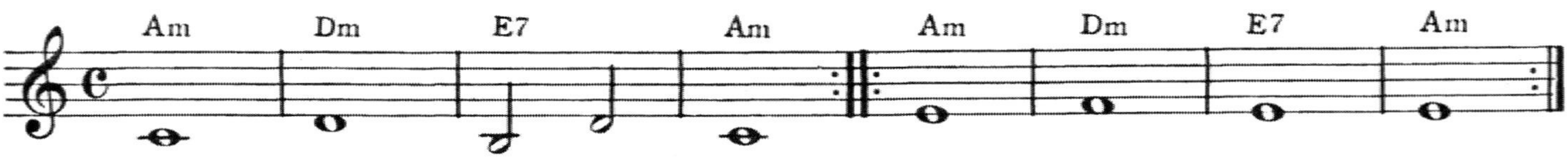


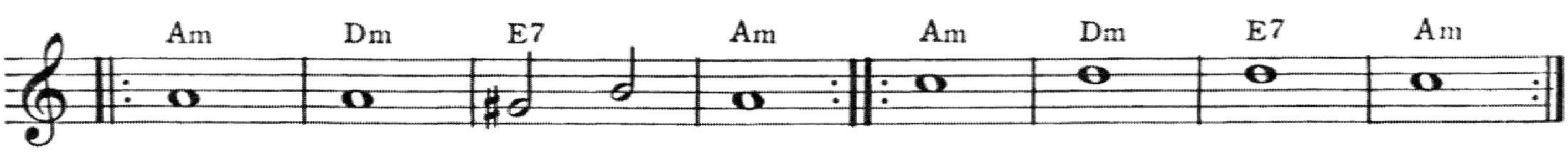


REPEAT USING PLAYING PATTERNS DESCRIBED ON PAGE SEVEN.

## THE HARMONIZED SCALE

(HARMONIC MODE)

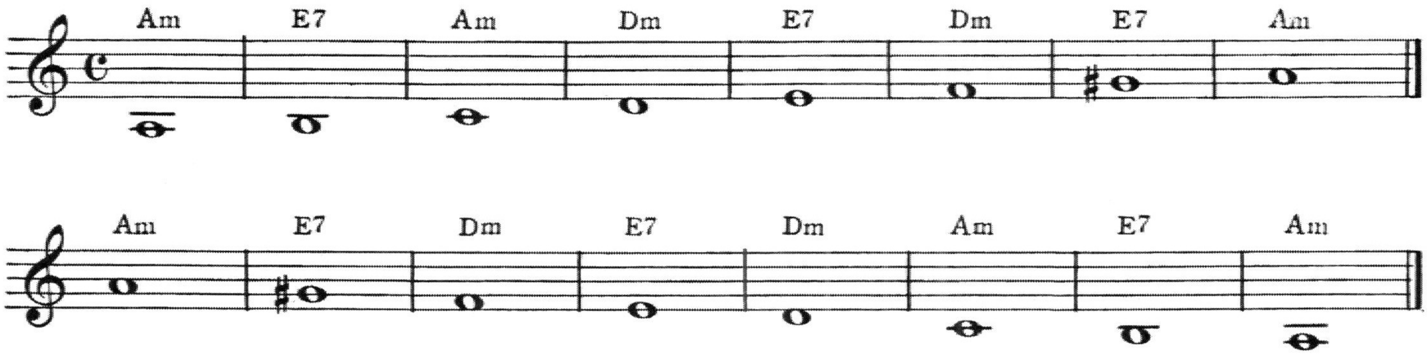


## NOCTURNE IN A MINOR

MEL BAY

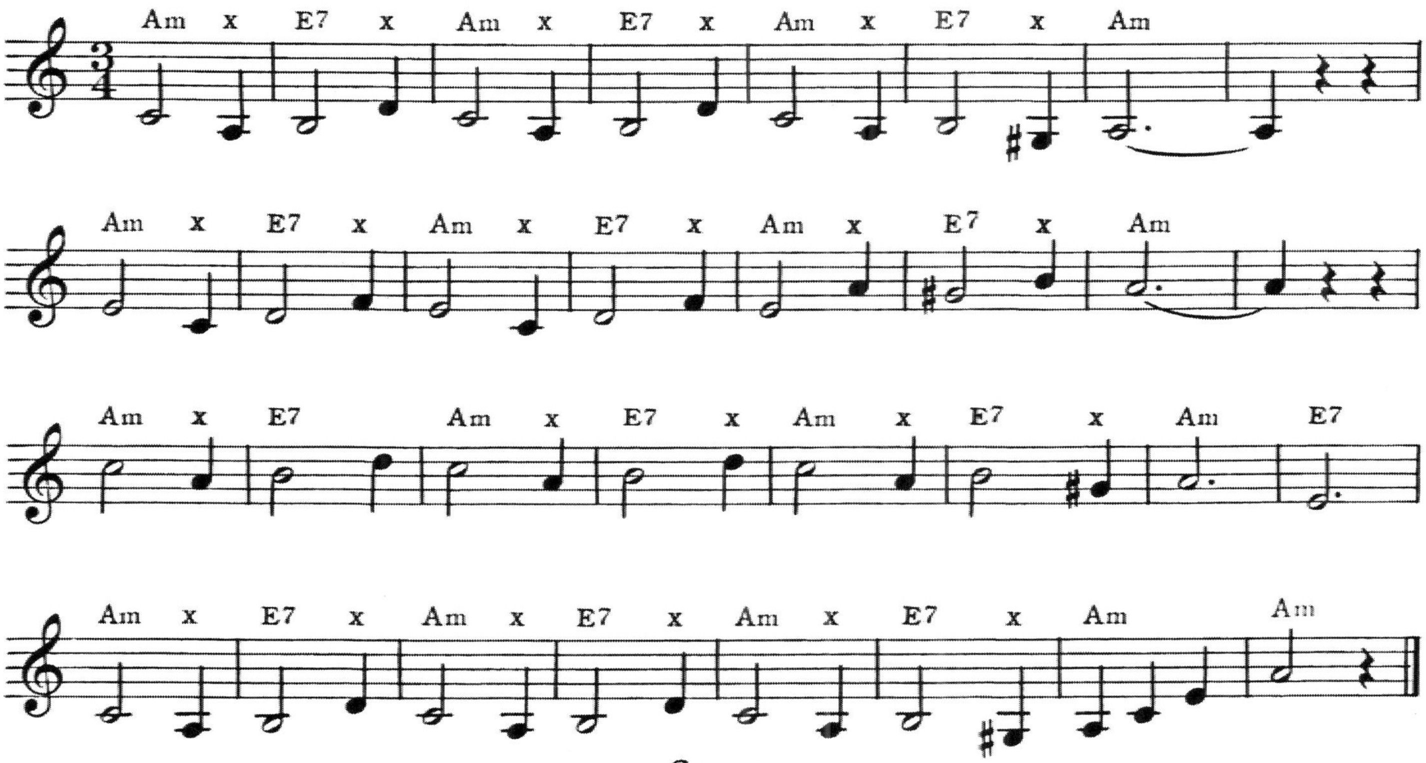


## Steps

A Half-Step is the distance from a given tone to the next higher or lower tone. On the Guitar the distance of a Half-Step is ONE FRET.

A Whole-Step consists of TWO Half-Steps.

The distance of a Whole-Step on the Guitar is TWO FRETS.

The C Scale has two half-steps. They are between E-F and B-C.

Note the distance of one fret between those notes. The distances between C-D, D-E, F-G, G-A, and A-B are Whole-Steps.

Whole-Steps and Half-Steps are also referred to as Whole-Tones and Half-Tones. We will refer to them as Whole-Steps and Half-Steps.

# HARMONIZING THE NON-CHORDAL TONES WITH THE Am CHORD

THE CHORDAL TONES OF THE Am CHORD ARE: A–C–E

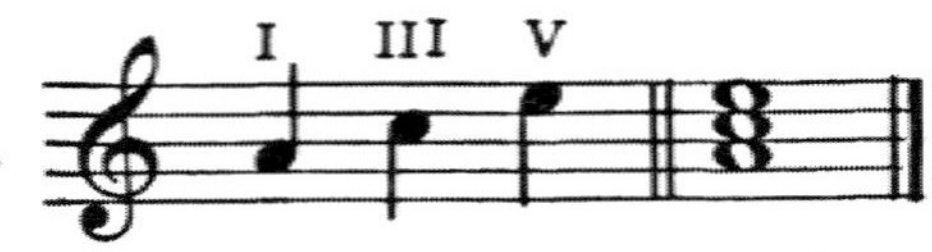


THE NON-CHORDAL TONES ARE: B–D–F–G

THE NON-CHORDAL TONES HARMONIZED WITH THE Am CHORD

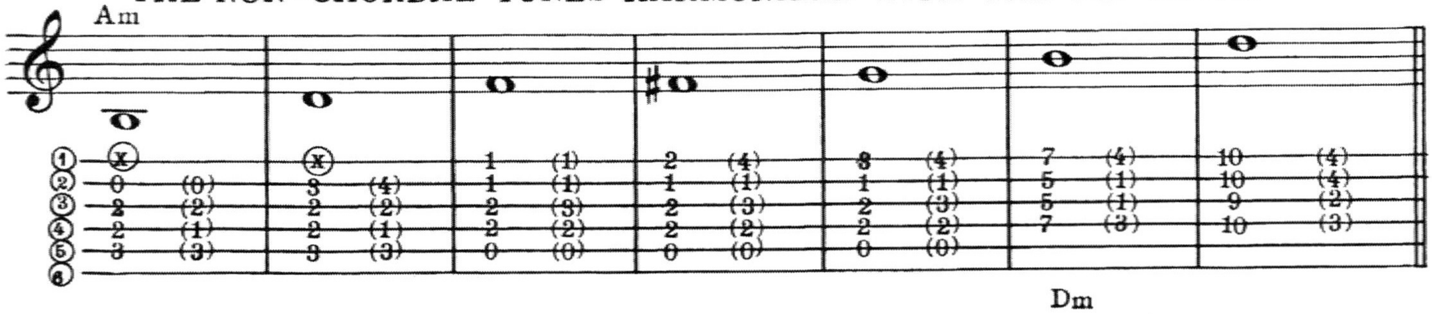


THE CHORDAL TONES ON THE Dm CHORD ARE: D–F–A

THE NON-CHORDAL TONES ARE: E–G–B–C

THE NON-CHORDAL TONES HARMONIZED WITH THE Dm CHORD

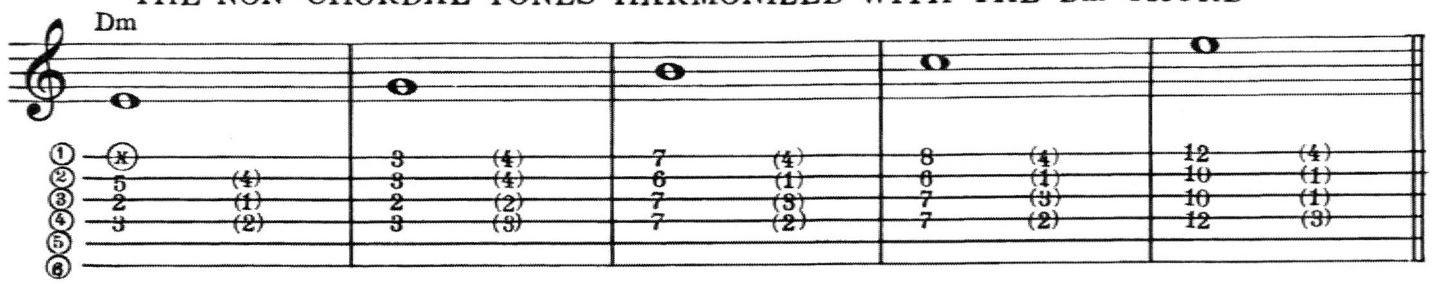


THE CHORDAL TONES OF THE E7 CHORD ARE: E–G♯–B–D

THE NON-CHORDAL TONES ARE: F–A–C

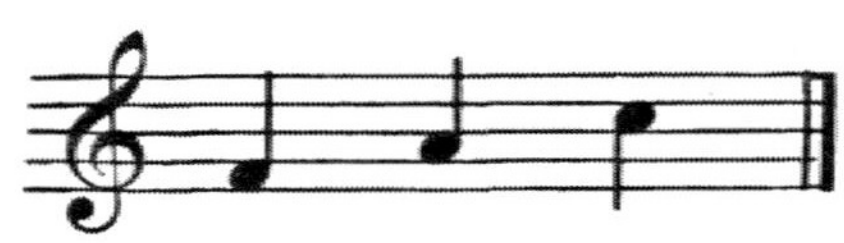

THE NON-CHORDAL TONES HARMONIZED WITH THE E7 CHORD

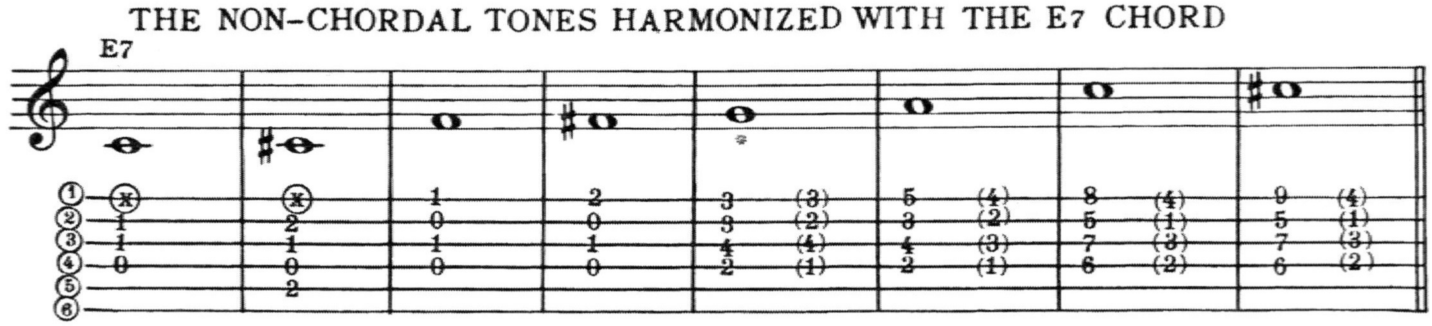

# The Key of C

All music studied so far in this book has been in the Key of C.

That means that the notes have been taken from the C Scale (shown below) and made into melodies.

It is called the C Scale because the first note is C and we proceed through the musical alphabet until C reappears. C-D-E-F-G-A-B-C.

We will cover the subject of keys and scales more thoroughly in the Theory and Harmony Chapters appearing later on in this course.

At present we will deal only with basic fundamentals.

## The C Scale

## The Key of A Minor
### (Relative to C Major)

Each Major key will have a Relative Minor key.

The Relative Minor Scale is built upon the *sixth tone* of the Major Scale.

The Key Signature of both will be the same.

The Minor Scale will have the same number of tones (7) as the Major.

The difference between the two scales is the arrangement of the Whole-Steps and Half-Steps.

### Harmonic

The 7th tone is raised one Half-Step ascending and descending.

### Melodic

The 6th and 7th tones are raised one half-step ascending and lowered back to their normal pitch descending.

### A NON-CHORDAL STUDY IN THE KEY OF A MINOR

# THE G CHORDS

Note the F♯ in the key signature

CHORD SPELLING: G-B-D

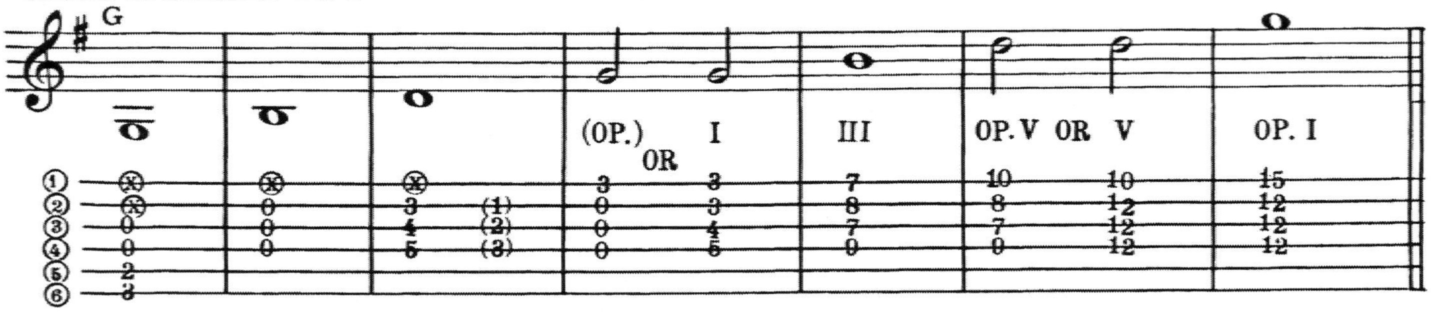


CHORD SPELLING: C-E-G

## THE C CHORDS

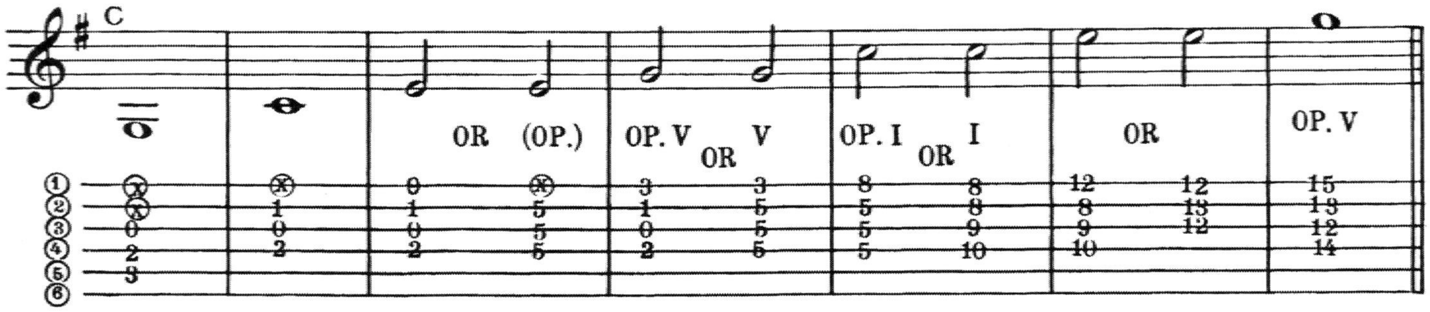


CHORD SPELLING: D-F♯-A-C

## THE D7 CHORDS

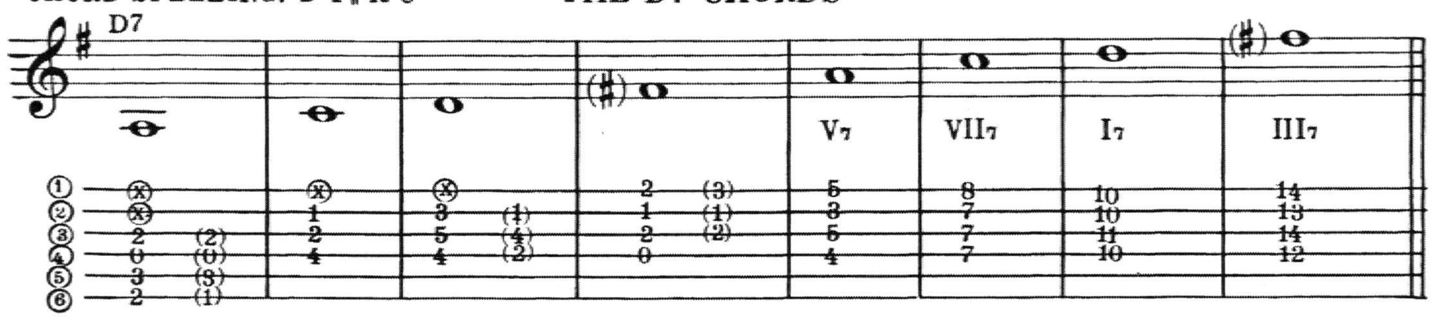


## A CHORD STUDY IN THE KEY OF G

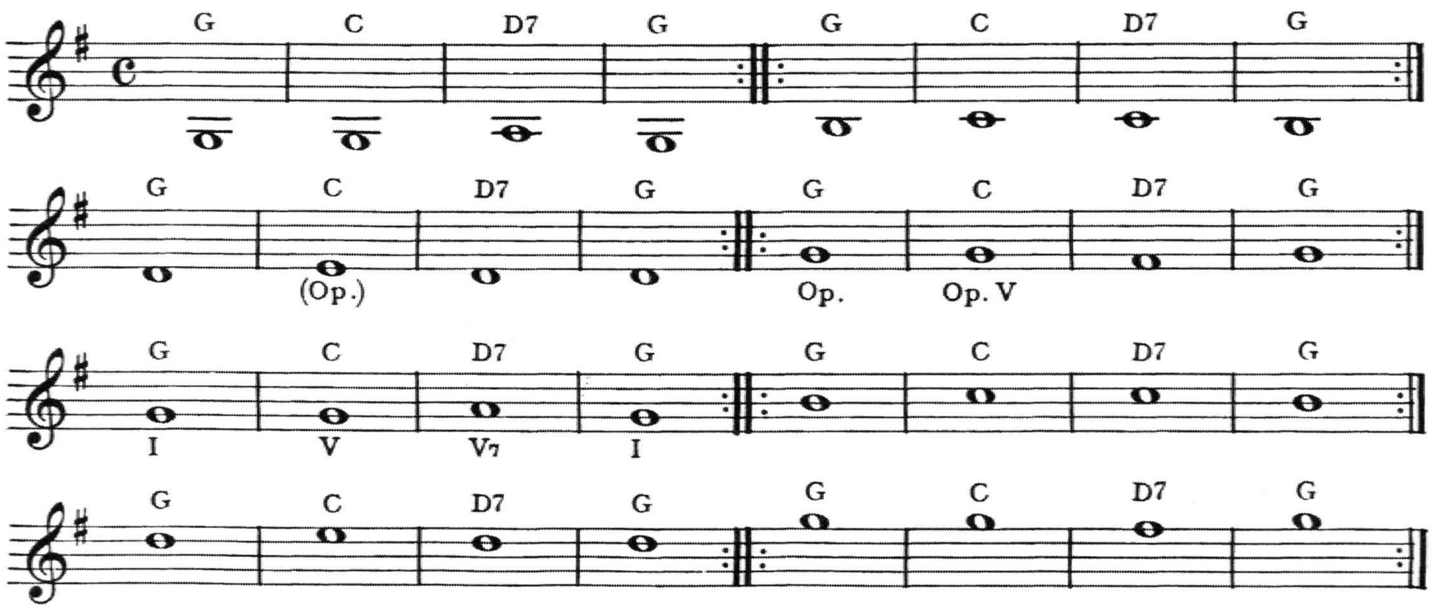

## HARMONIZING THE G SCALE

(TWO OCTAVES)

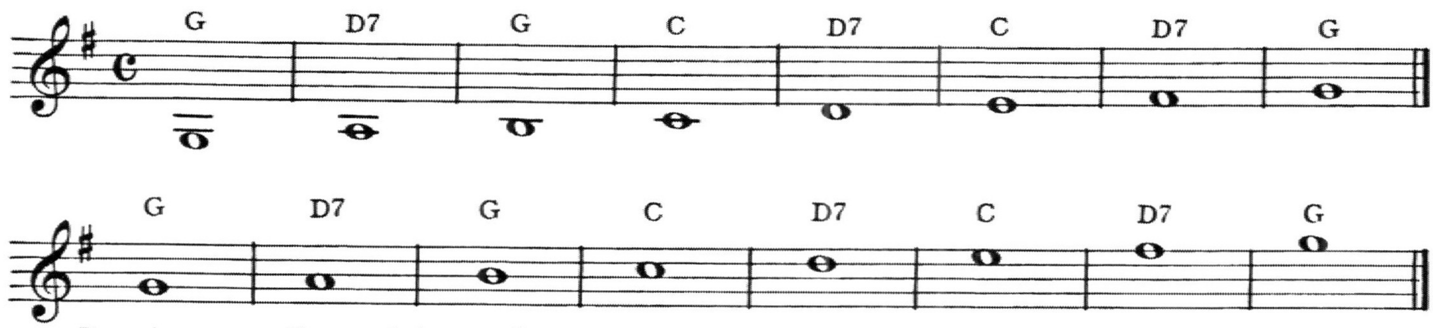


Practice ascending and descending.

## SHE'LL BE COMIN' ROUND THE MOUNTAIN

## HAND ME DOWN MY WALKING CANE

## HARMONIZING THE NON-CHORDAL TONES WITH THE G CHORD

THE CHORDAL TONES OF THE G CHORD ARE: G–B–D

THE NON-CHORDAL TONES ARE: A–C–E–F♯

### HARMONIZING THE NON-CHORDAL TONES WITH THE G CHORD

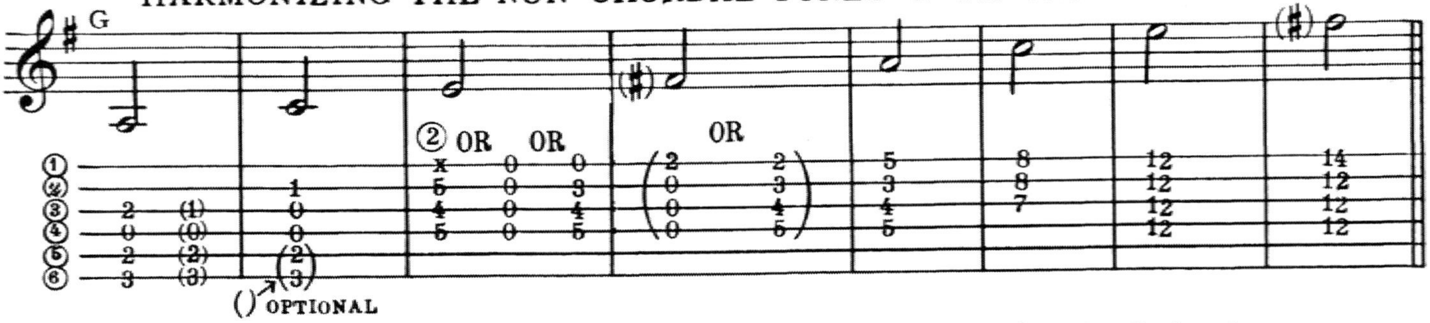


See page 10 for harmonizing the Non-Chordal tones with the C chord.

ONE EXCEPTION WILL BE THE F♯ NOTE. THIS NOTE WILL HARMONIZE IN THIS MANNER:

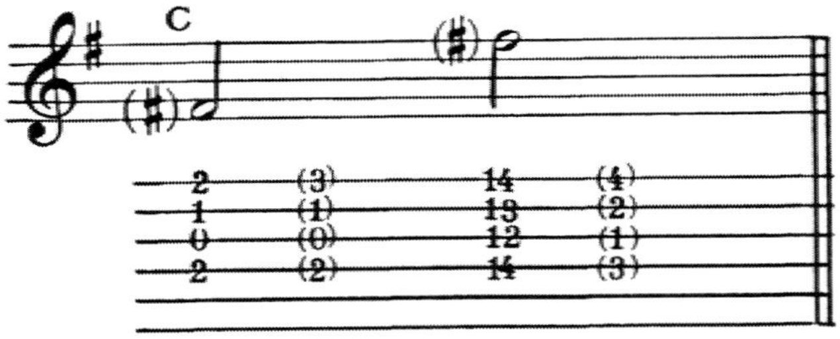


THE CHORDAL TONES OF THE D7 CHORD ARE: D-F♯-A-C

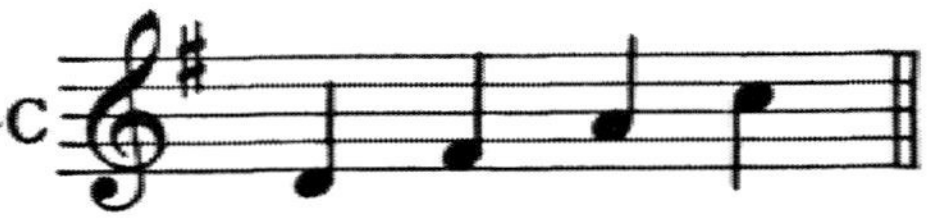

THE NON-CHORDAL TONES OF THE D7 CHORD ARE: E-G-B

### HARMONIZING THE NON-CHORDAL TONES WITH THE D7 CHORD

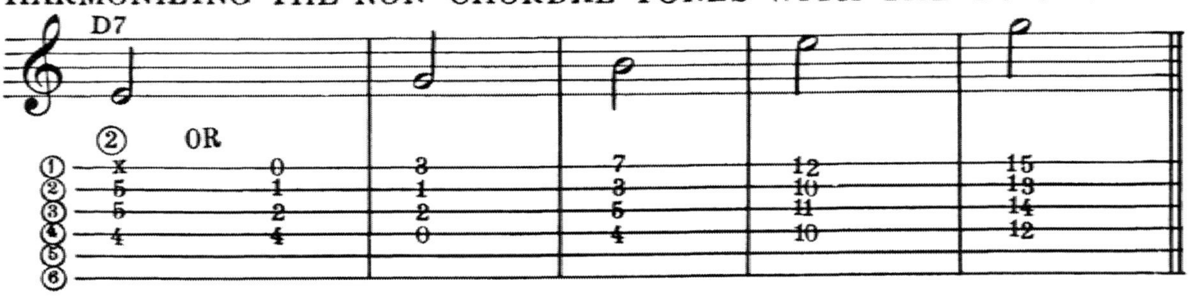


### MELODY IN G WITH NON-CHORDAL TONES

D.C. al Fine: Go back to beginning to Fine.

*D. C. al Fine*

## THE MELODY CHORDS IN THE KEY OF E MINOR

(Relative to the key of G)

The chords in the key of E Minor are: Em, Am and B7

### THE E MINOR CHORDS

Symbol: Em
Spelling: E–G–B

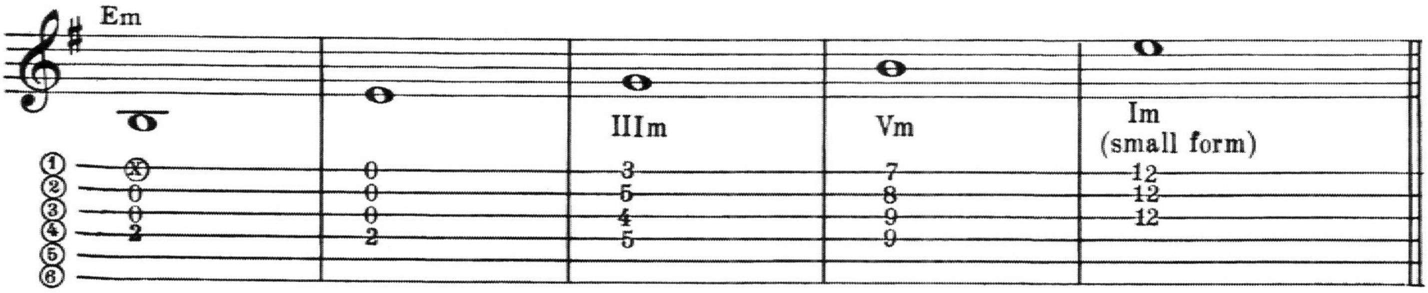


### THE A MINOR CHORDS

See page fourteen for the complete review of the Am chords necessary for the mastery of this chapter.

### THE B7 CHORDS

Symbol: B7
Chord Spelling: B–D♯–F♯–A

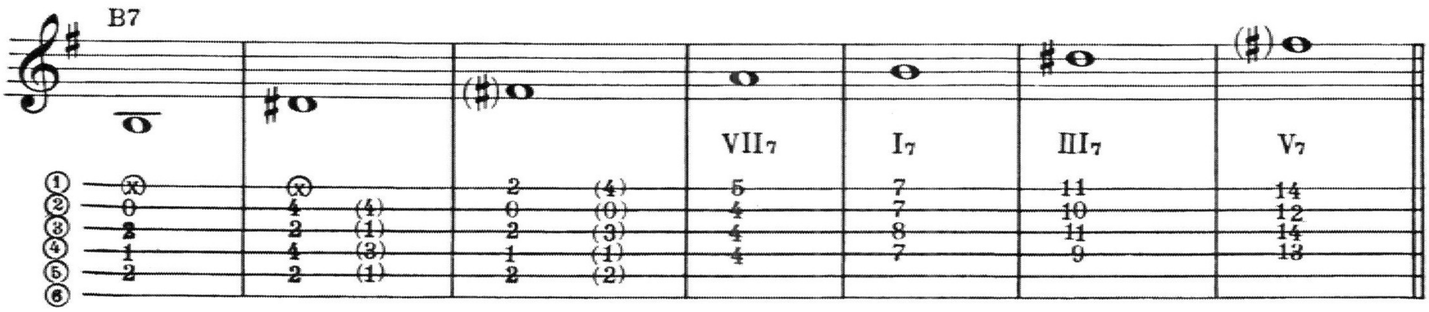


### MELODY CHORD STUDY IN E MINOR

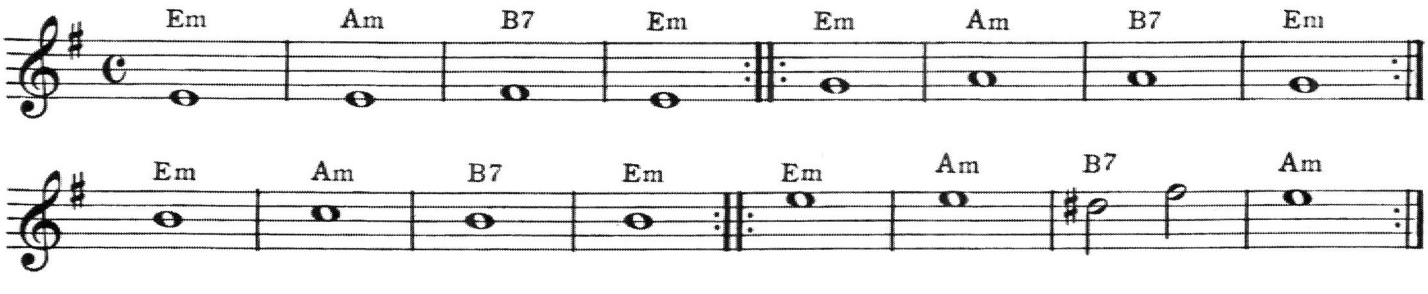


### THE HARMONIZED SCALE

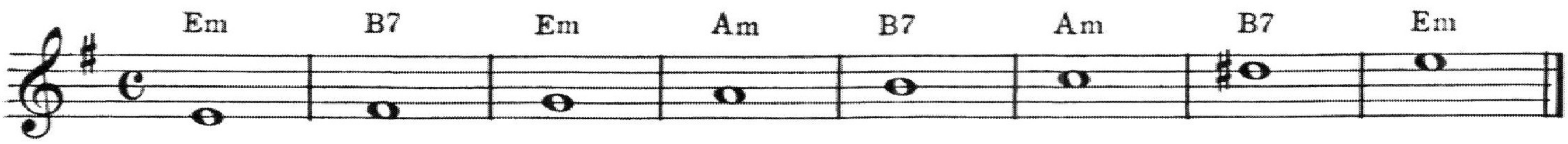


Practice ascending and descending.

## PLAYING EIGHTH NOTES

The best way to play melody chords in a passage containing eighth notes is to play the chords on the beats with the following eighth notes being played as single notes.

EXAMPLE:

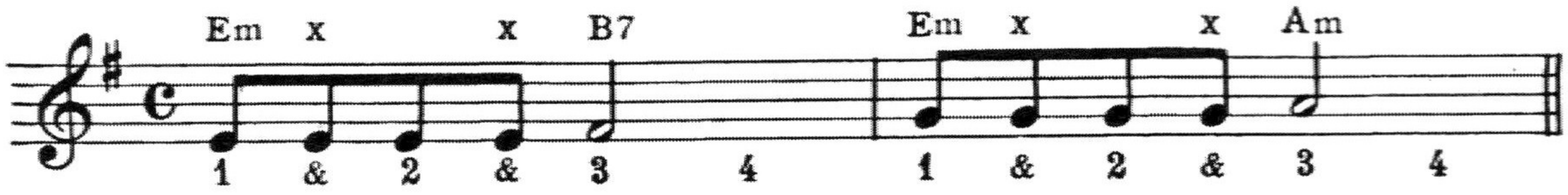


## THE HOPE
### (HATIK VOH)

## SOMETIMES I FEEL LIKE A MOTHERLESS CHILD

## HARMONIZING THE NON-CHORDAL TONES WITH THE Em CHORD

THE NON-CHORDAL TONES HARMONIZED WITH THE Em CHORD

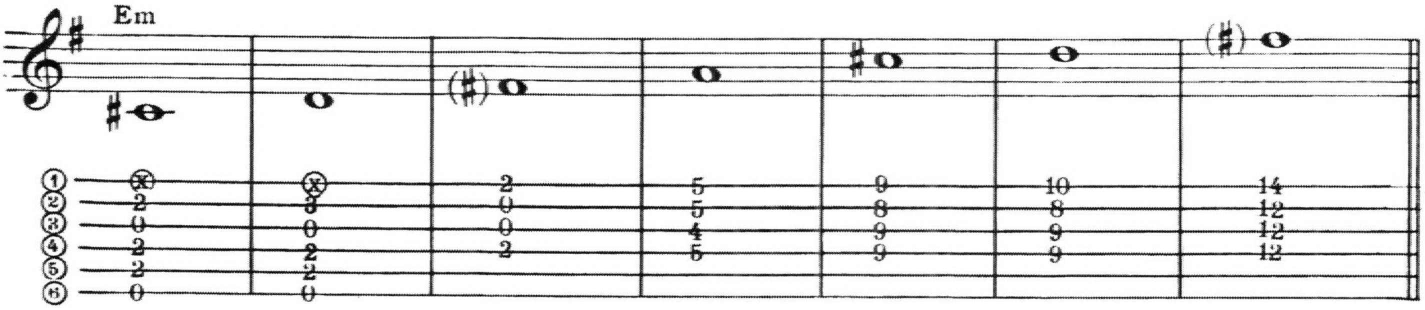


See page sixteen for the Non-Chordal tones harmonized with the Am chord.

### HARMONIZING THE NON-CHORDAL TONES WITH THE B7 CHORD

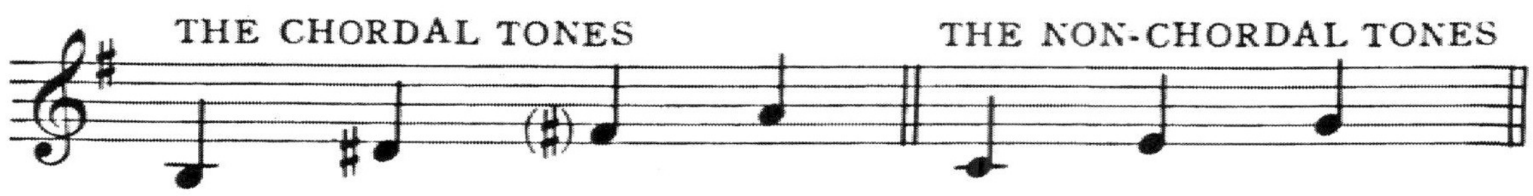


THE NON-CHORDAL TONES HARMONIZED WITH THE B7 CHORD

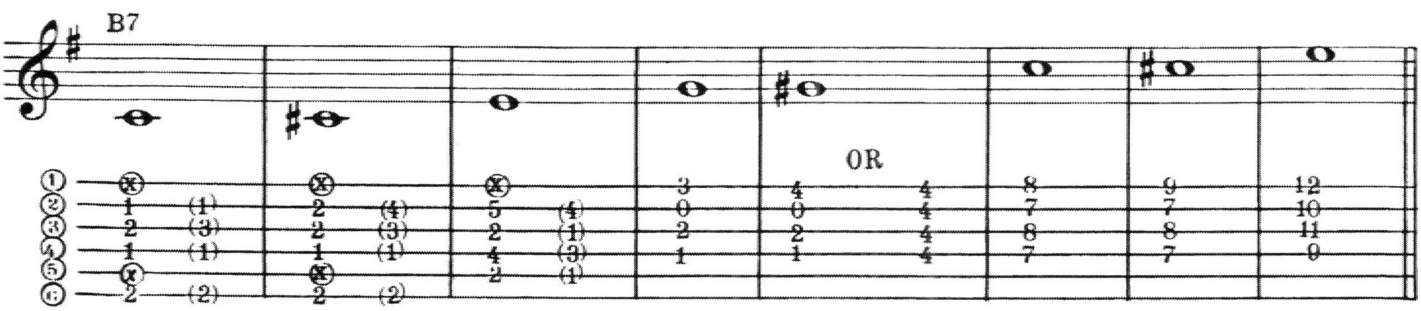


### NON-CHORDAL STUDY IN E MINOR

# THE WAYFARIN' STRANGER

## The Technical Names of the Scale Steps

Each degree of the scale will be designated by a number and a specific technical name. Up to this point in this course we have referred only to the letter name of each degree depending on the note falling on each degree. The number of each scale degree will be in Roman numerals.

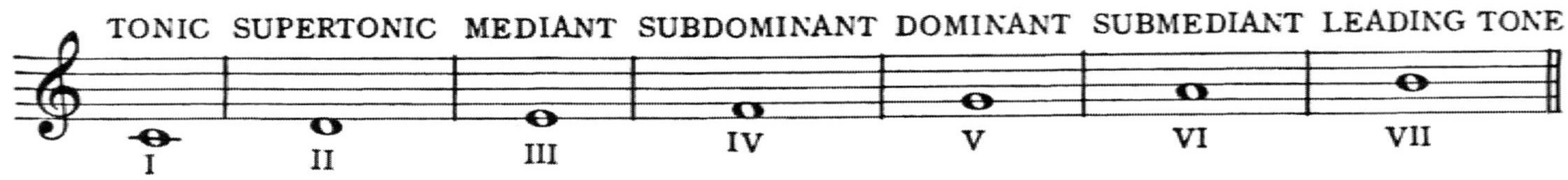


## The Chromatic Scale

The Chromatic Scale is composed of *twelve Half-Steps* within an octave.

It may be written from any pitch; the Key-Signature will be that of the Major Key of the chosen pitch. It is written upward in sharps and downward in flats.

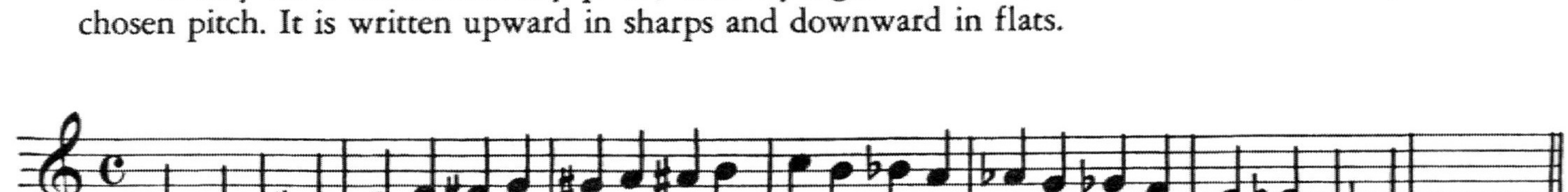

# THE MELODY CHORDS IN THE KEY OF F

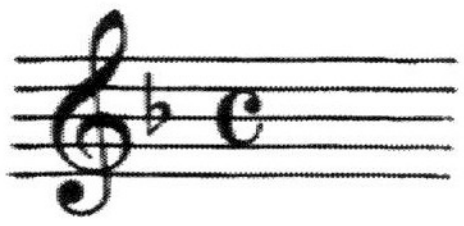

The key signature for the key of F
All B notes will be played flat.

THE CHORDS IN THE KEY OF F ARE F, B♭ AND C7

CHORD SPELLING: F-A-C

## THE F CHORDS

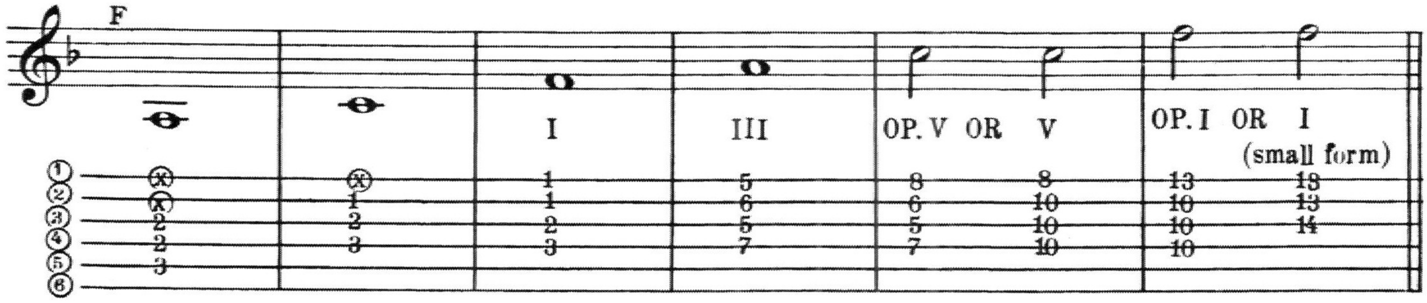


SYMBOL: B♭
CHORD SPELLING: B♭-D-F

## THE B-flat CHORDS

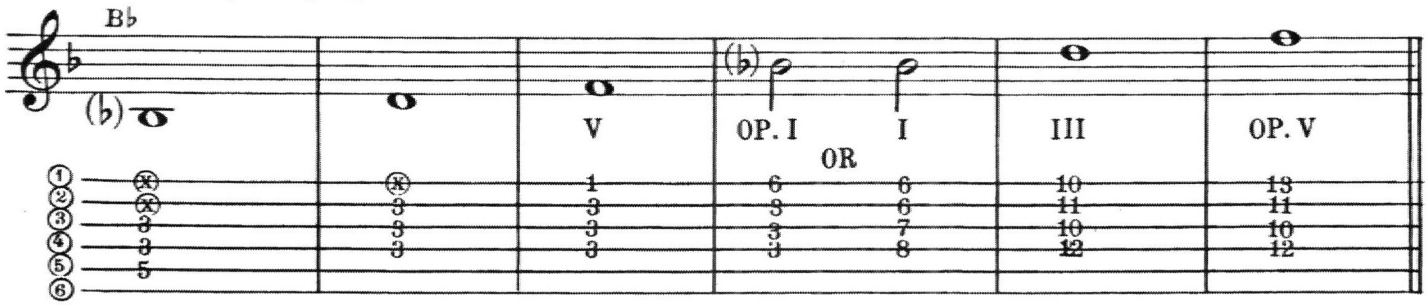


CHORD SPELLING: C-E-G-B♭

## THE C7 CHORDS

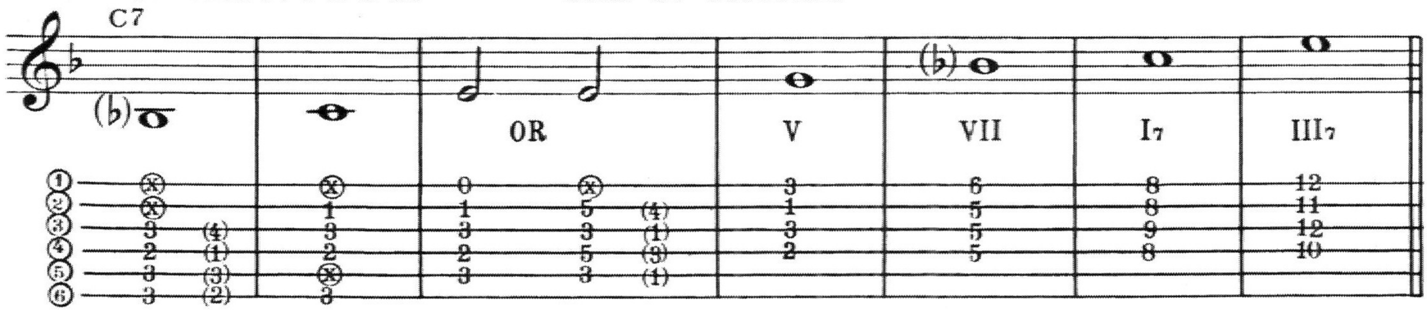


## CHORD STUDY IN THE KEY OF F

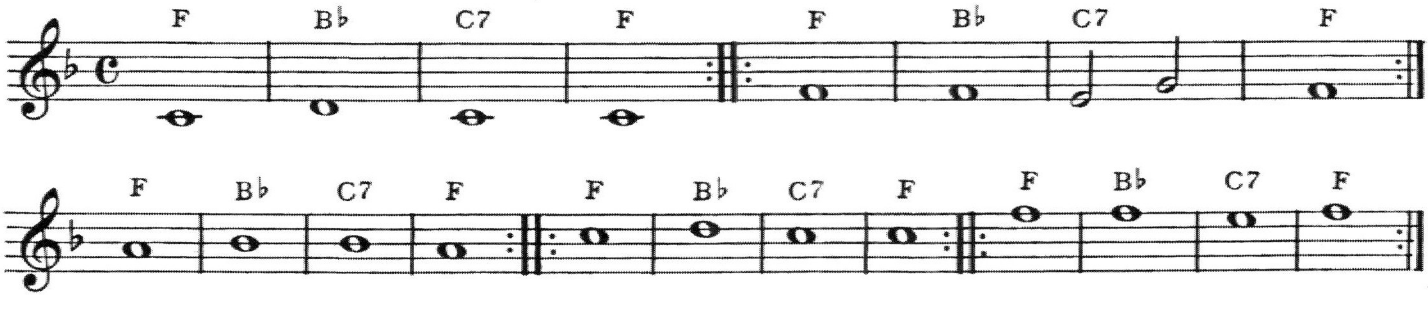

## THE HARMONIZED SCALE

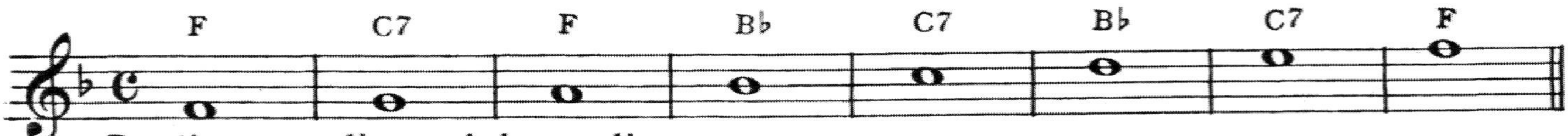


Practice ascending and descending.

## AUNT RHODY

## CARELESS LOVE

## Intervals

An INTERVAL is the distance between two tones or the difference in pitch between two tones when sounded.

Intervals are measured *upward* from the lower tone to the higher.

Intervals have NUMBER names and TYPE names. For example a 3rd could be major or minor depending upon the distance.

The staff degree occupied by the lower note and the staff degree occupied by the higher note are *both included* when determining the number name of the interval.

Below are nine intervals from C to each note in the C Scale.

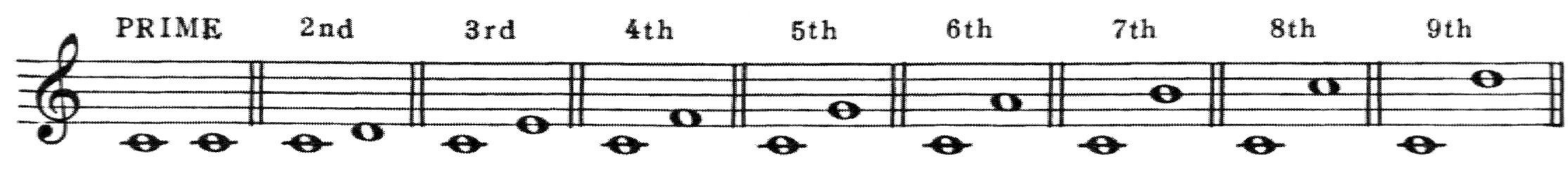

## HARMONIZING THE NON-CHORDAL TONES WITH THE F CHORD

THE CHORDAL TONES THE NON-CHORDAL TONES

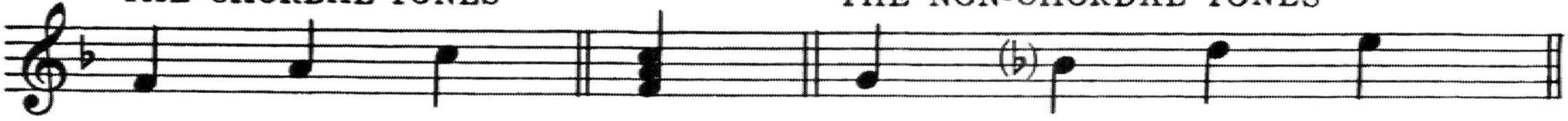

THE NON-CHORDAL TONES HARMONIZED WITH THE F CHORD

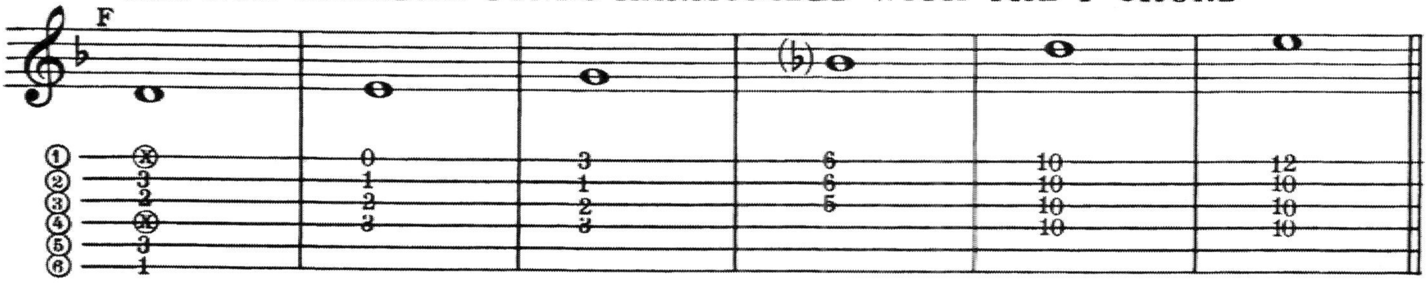


## HARMONIZING THE NON-CHORDAL TONES WITH THE B♭ CHORD

THE CHORDAL TONES THE NON-CHORDAL TONES

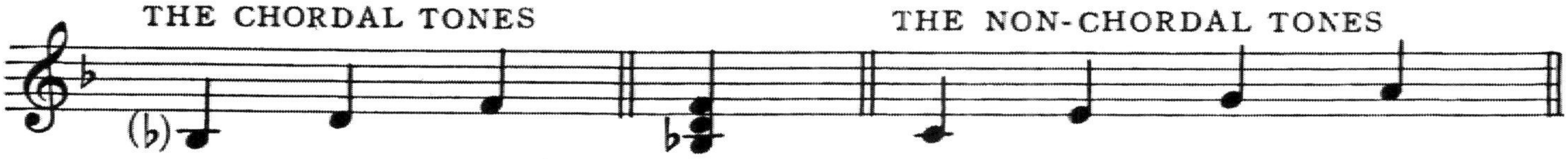

THE NON-CHORDAL TONES HARMONIZED WITH THE B♭ CHORDS

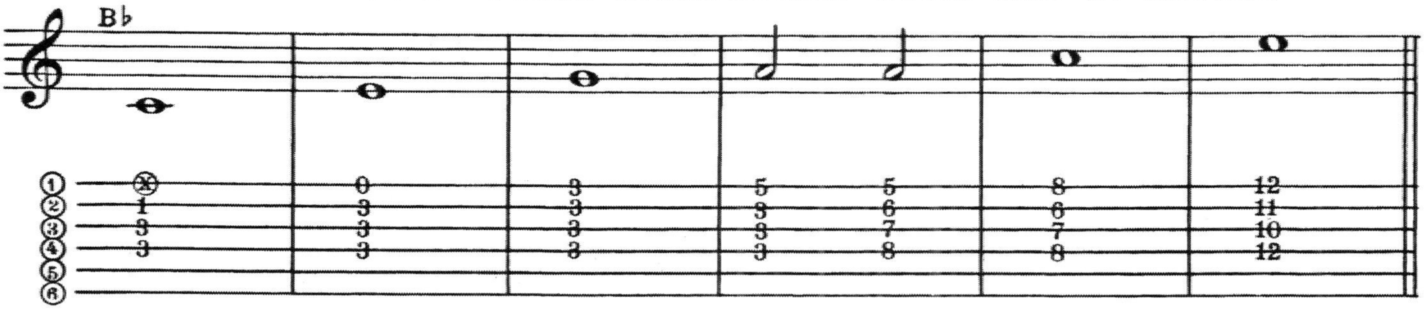


## HARMONIZING THE NON-CHORDAL TONES WITH THE C7 CHORD

THE CHORDAL TONES THE NON-CHORDAL TONES

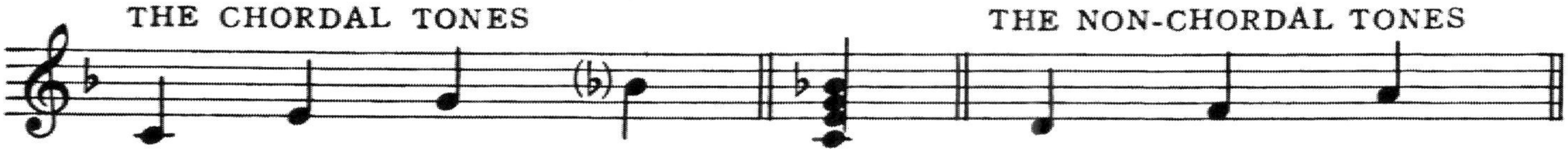

THE NON-CHORDAL TONES HARMONIZED WITH THE C7 CHORD

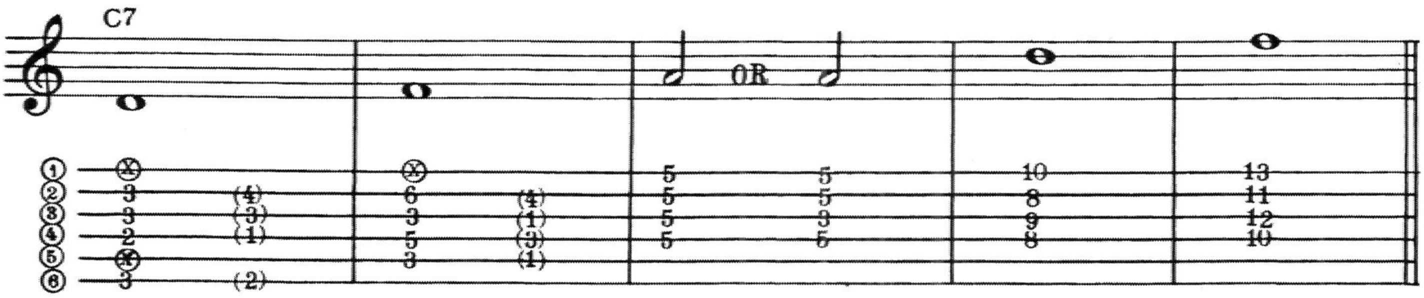

# THE MELODY CHORDS IN THE KEY OF D MINOR

RELATIVE TO F MAJOR

SYMBOL: Dm
CHORD SPELLING: D-F-A

## THE D MINOR CHORDS

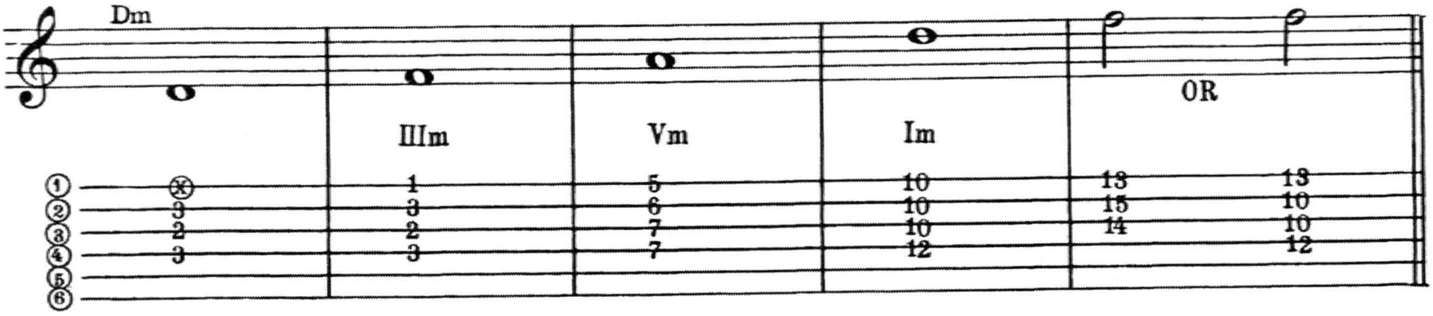


CHORD SPELLING: G-B♭-D

## THE G MINOR CHORDS

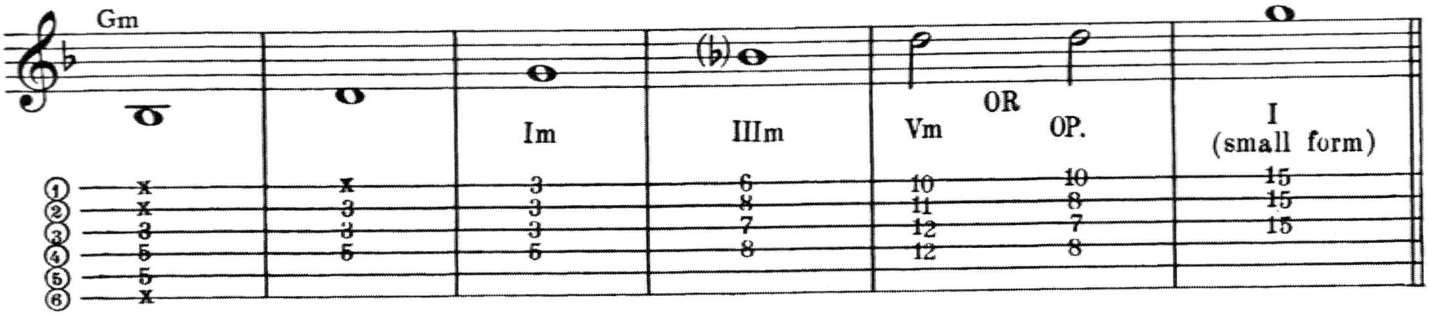


CHORD SPELLING: A-C♯-E-G

## THE A7 CHORDS

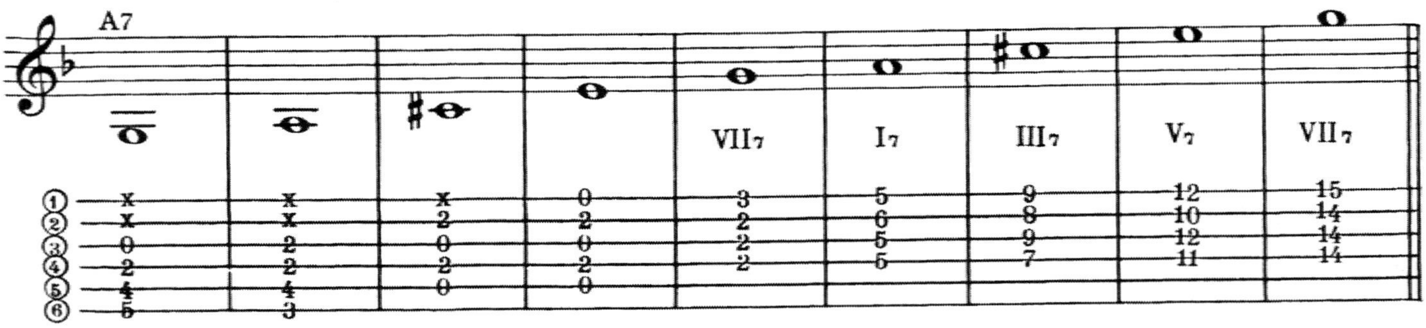


## CHORD STUDY

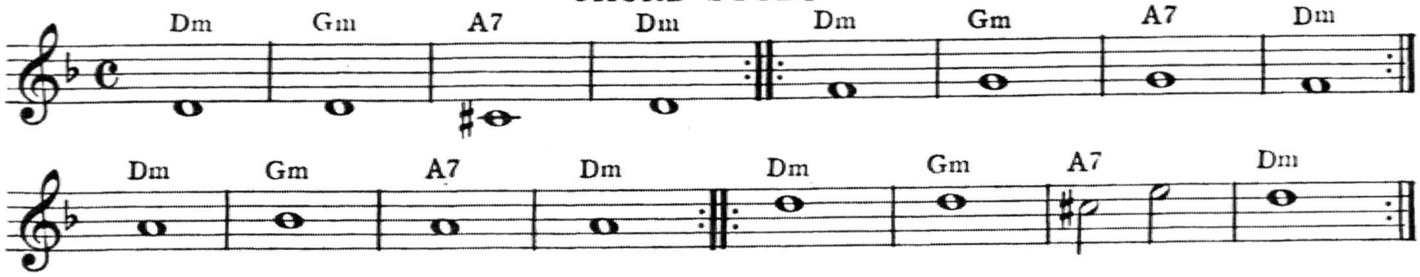


## THE HARMONIZED SCALE

Practice ascending and descending.

# BLACK IS THE COLOR OF MY TRUE LOVE'S HAIR

* Note that this single note passage is played on the 3rd string, 7th fret, 2nd string, 6th fret and 1st sting, 5th fret.

# AURA LEE

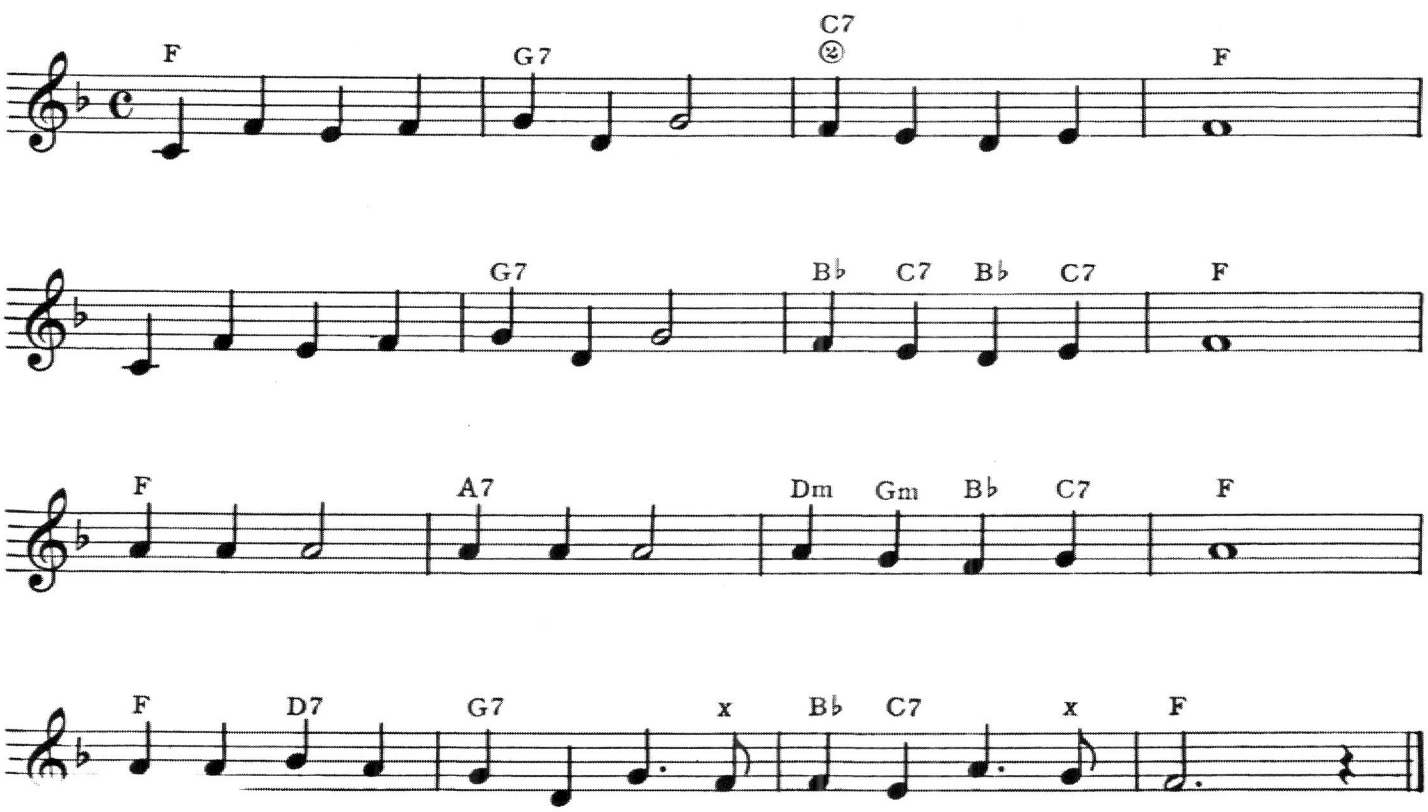

## HARMONIZING THE NON-CHORDAL TONES WITH THE Dm CHORD

THE CHORDAL TONES

THE NON-CHORDAL TONES

### HARMONIZING THE NON-CHORDAL TONES

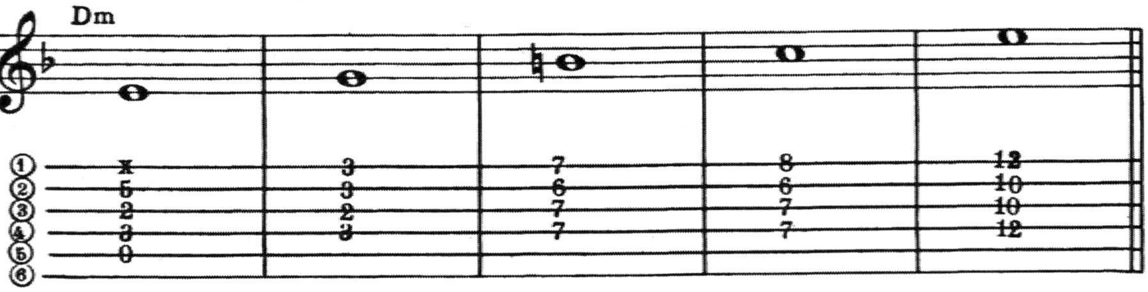


## HARMONIZING THE NON-CHORDAL TONES WITH THE Gm CHORD

THE CHORDAL TONES

THE NON-CHORDAL TONES

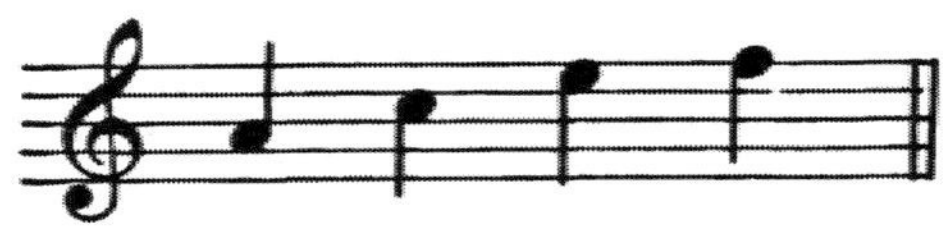

### THE NON-CHORDAL TONES HARMONIZED

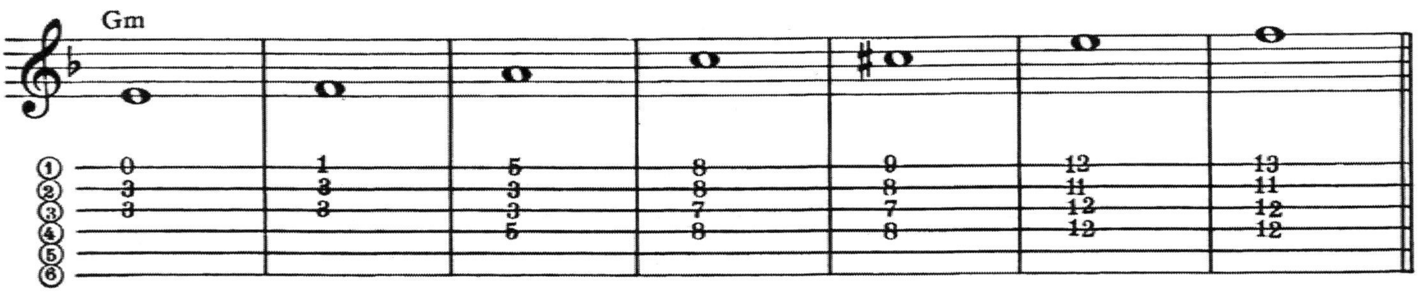


## HARMONIZING THE NON-CHORDAL TONES WITH THE A7 CHORD

THE CHORDAL TONES

THE NON-CHORDAL TONES

### THE NON-CHORDAL TONES HARMONIZED

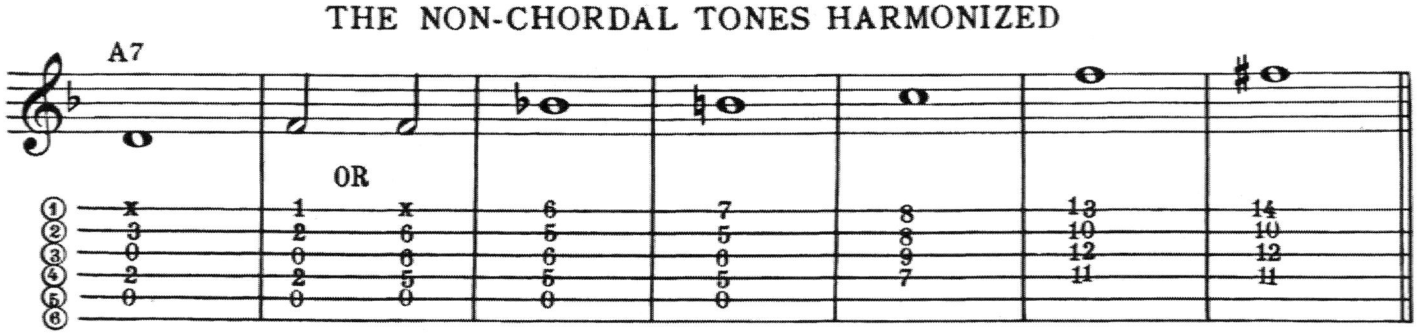

# A NON-CHORDAL STUDY IN D MINOR

For good effect play the notes ( ) in the following solo as follows: 8 below the note: play an octave lower.

## DARK EYES

# THE DIMINISHED CHORDS

This chord is different from all other chords in that any note of the chord may be the root. Although it is one of the most important chords in music it belongs to no key relationship. There are three principal groups of diminished chords. There is one principal form employed on the top four strings. Although there are several ways of obtaining diminished chords, we will employ one principal outside form and one basic inside form for this text. For other forms see the Mel Bay Method For the Modern Guitar. The Mel Bay Chord System For Rhythm And Orchestral Guitar will show the best diminished forms for rhythm work.

The Diminished Forms

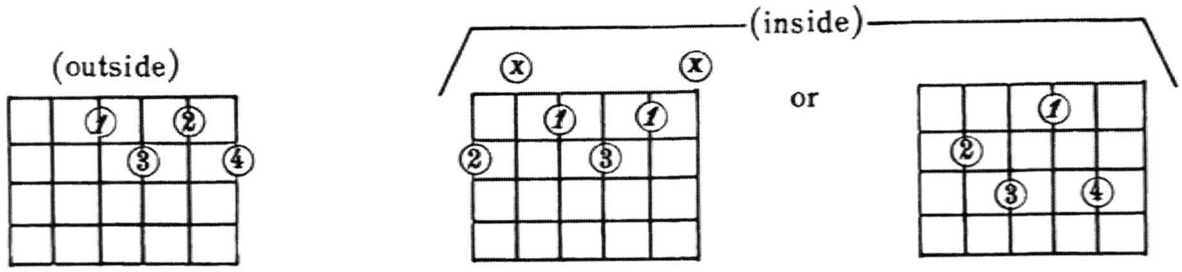


Symbol for diminished is: dim. or –. Sometimes you will see this (○) small zero used. Most modern arrangers employ the minus (–) sign.

DIMINISHED SET NUMBER ONE

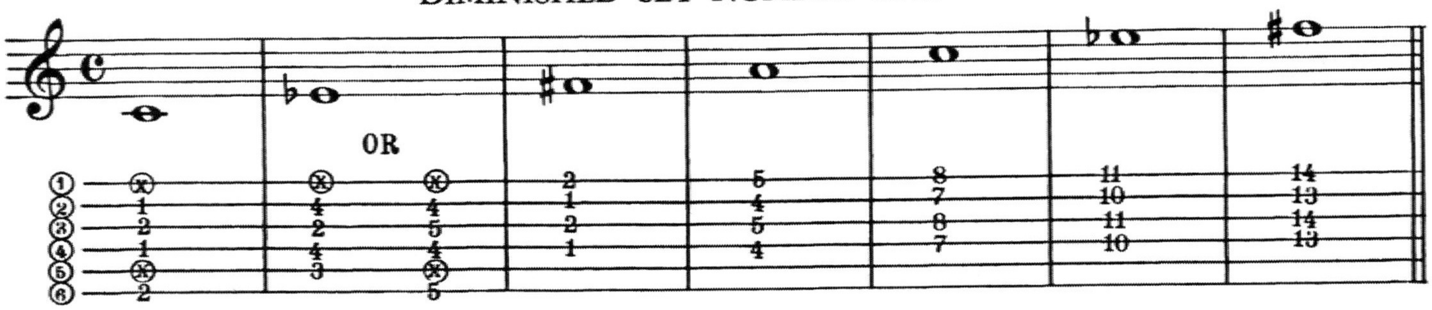


DIMINISHED SET NUMBER TWO

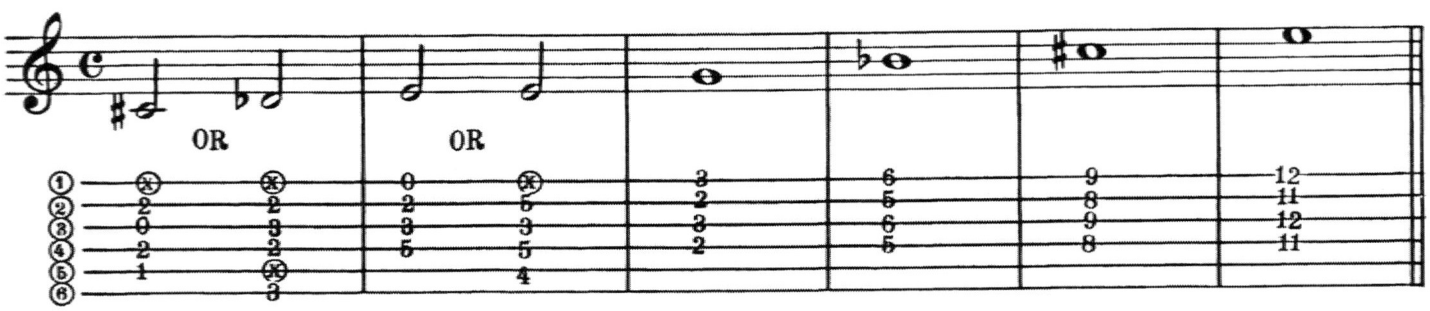


DIMINISHED SET NUMBER THREE

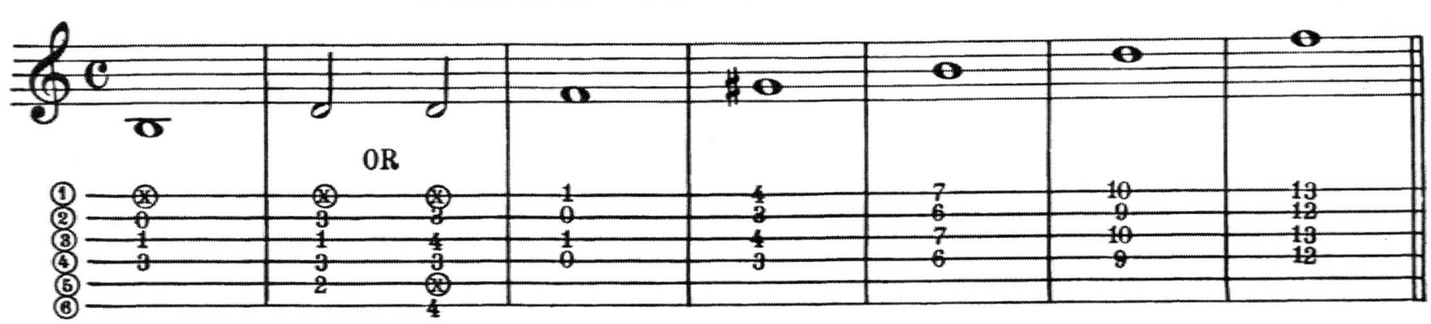

# THE NON-CHORDAL TONES HARMONIZED WITH THE DIMINISHED CHORDS

OUTSIDE FORM

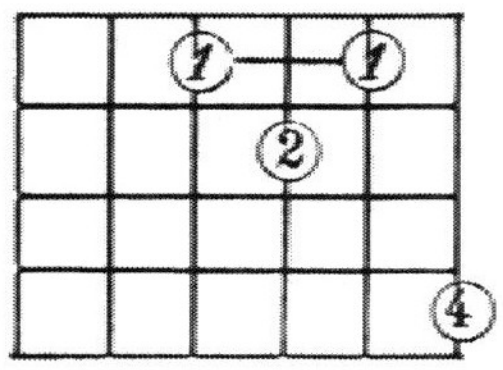

INSIDE FORM

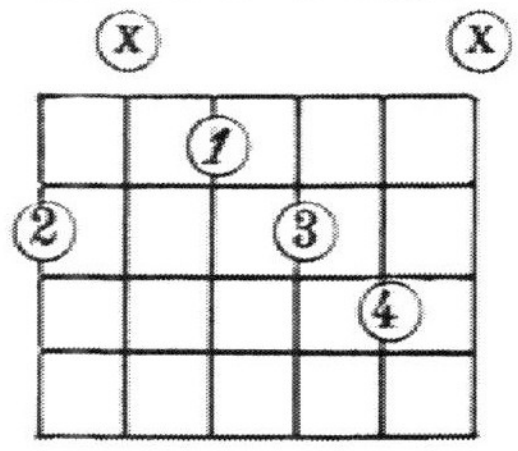

SET ONE WITH NON-CHORDAL TONES

SET TWO WITH NON-CHORDAL TONES

SET THREE WITH NON-CHORDAL TONES

# THE AUGMENTED CHORD

SYMBOL: Aug or (+)  The plus sign is the most commonly used symbol.

Theoretically speaking, augmented chords are produced by raising the fifth tone of the major chord one-half step. Since we do not delve in harmony, Grade Four of the Mel Bay Modern Guitar Method gives a complete chapter on that subject.
Like the diminished chords, the augmented chord will consist of one principal outside form and one main inside form as shown below.

(outside form)

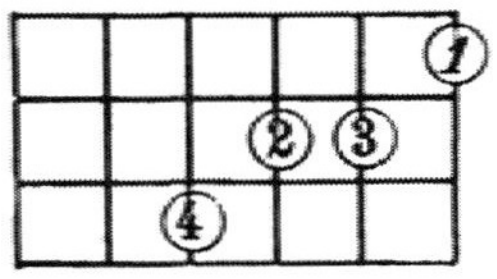

(inside form)

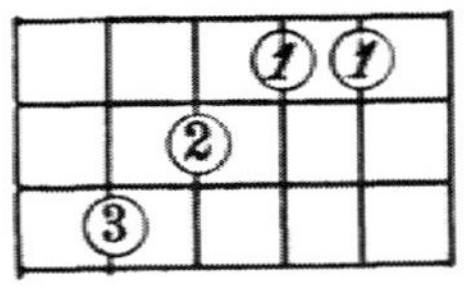

GROUP ONE

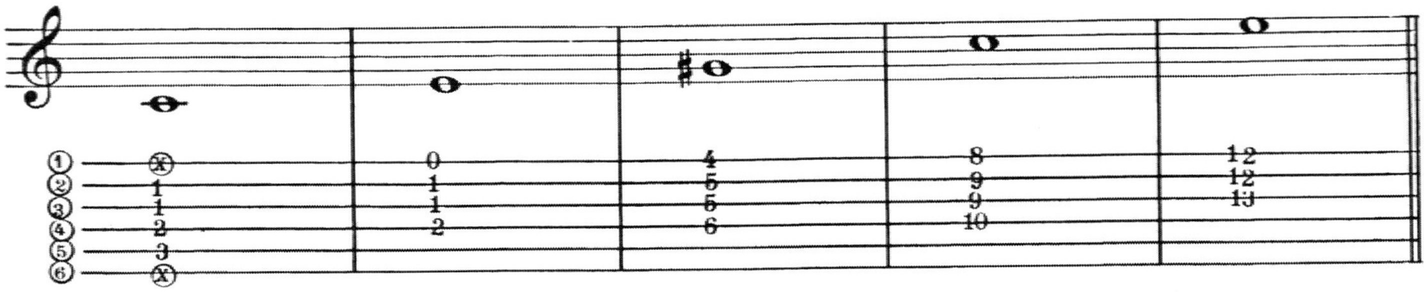

GROUP TWO

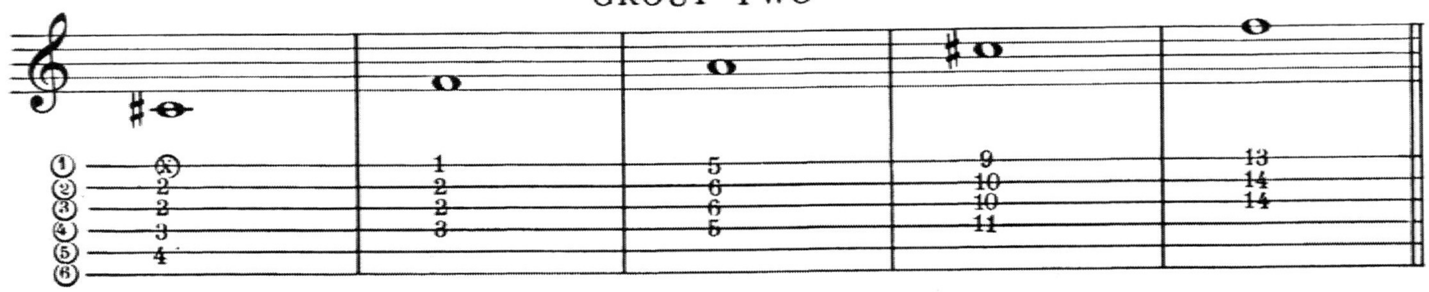

GROUP THREE

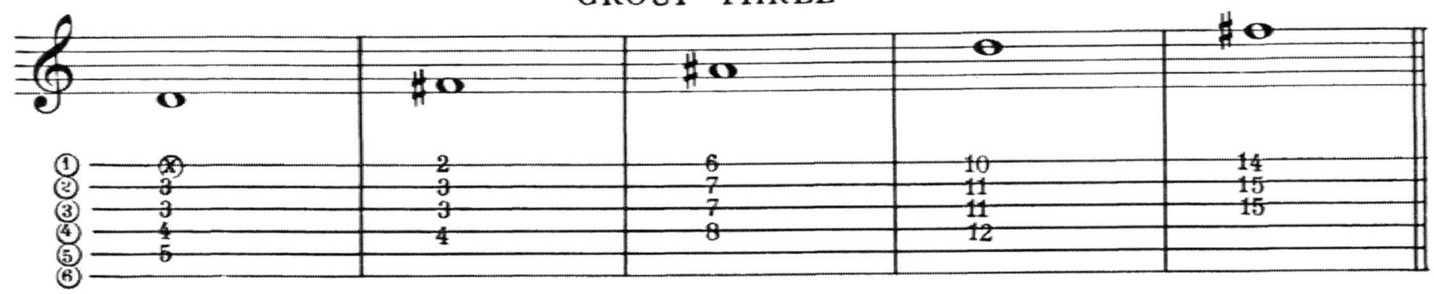

GROUP FOUR

# HARMONIZING THE NON-CHORAL TONES WITH THE AUGMENTED CHORDS

## GROUP ONE

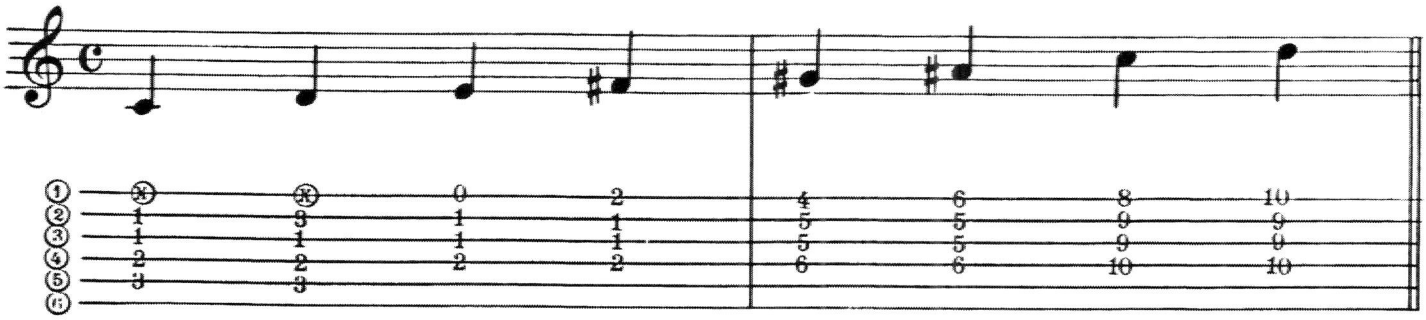

## GROUP TWO

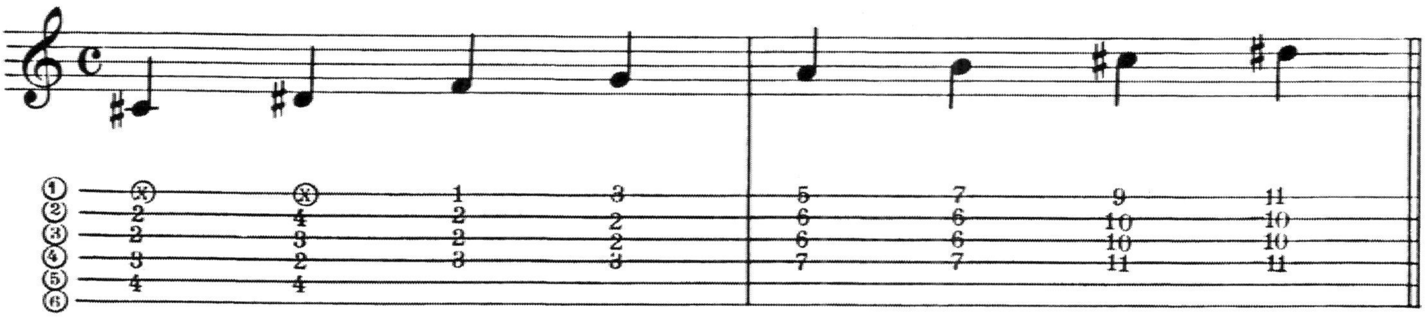

## GROUP THREE

## GROUP FOUR

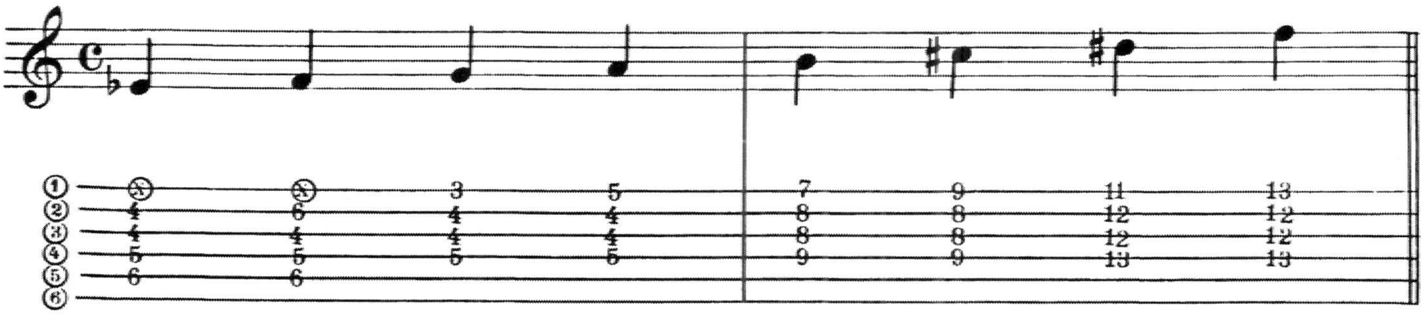

# THE MELODY CHORDS IN THE KEY OF D MAJOR

The chords in the key of D major are D, G and A7

## THE D CHORDS

CHORD SPELLING: D-F♯-A

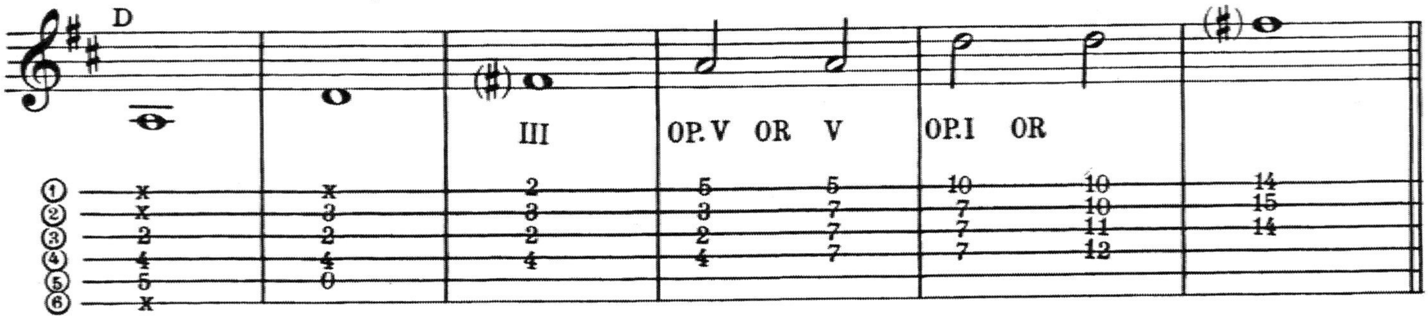


## THE G CHORDS

CHORD SPELLING: G-B-D

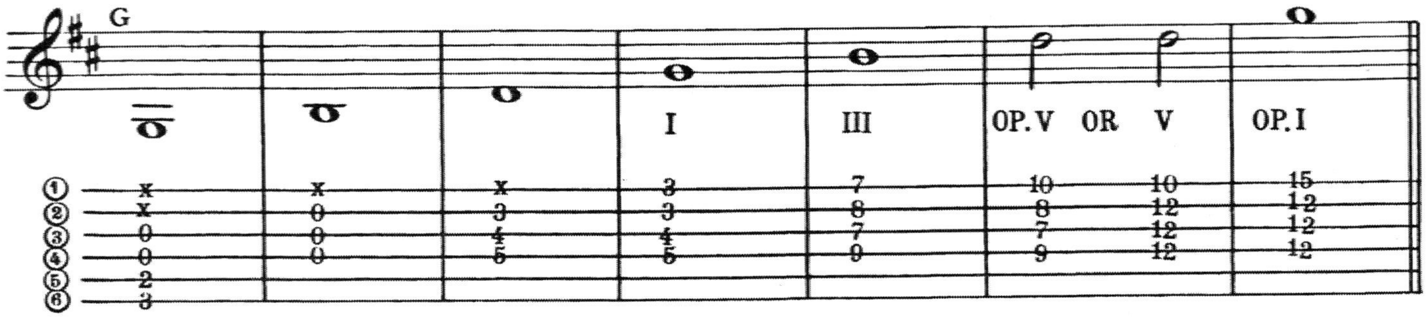


## THE A7 CHORDS

CHORD SPELLING: A-C♯-E-G

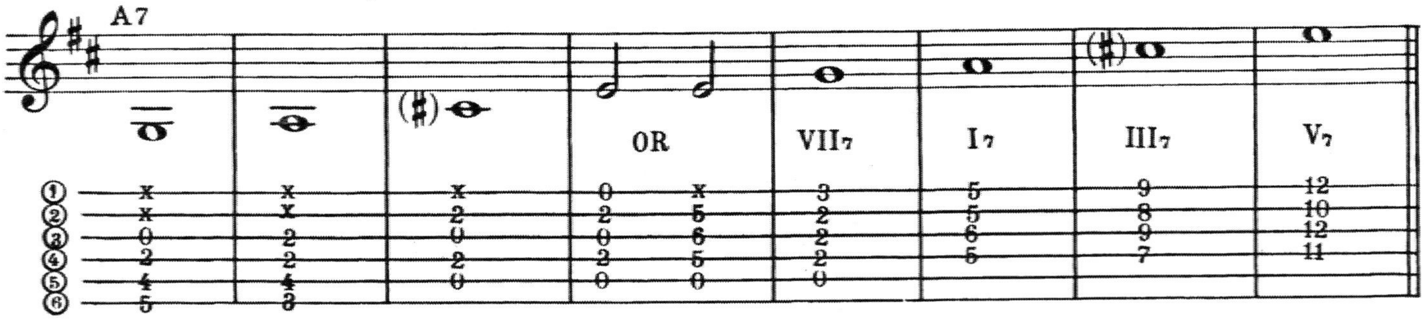


## CHORD STUDY

## THE D SCALE HARMONIZED

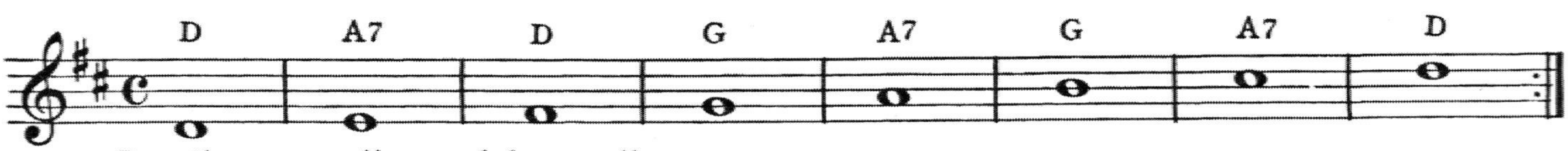


Practice ascending and descending.

## THE STREETS OF LAREDO

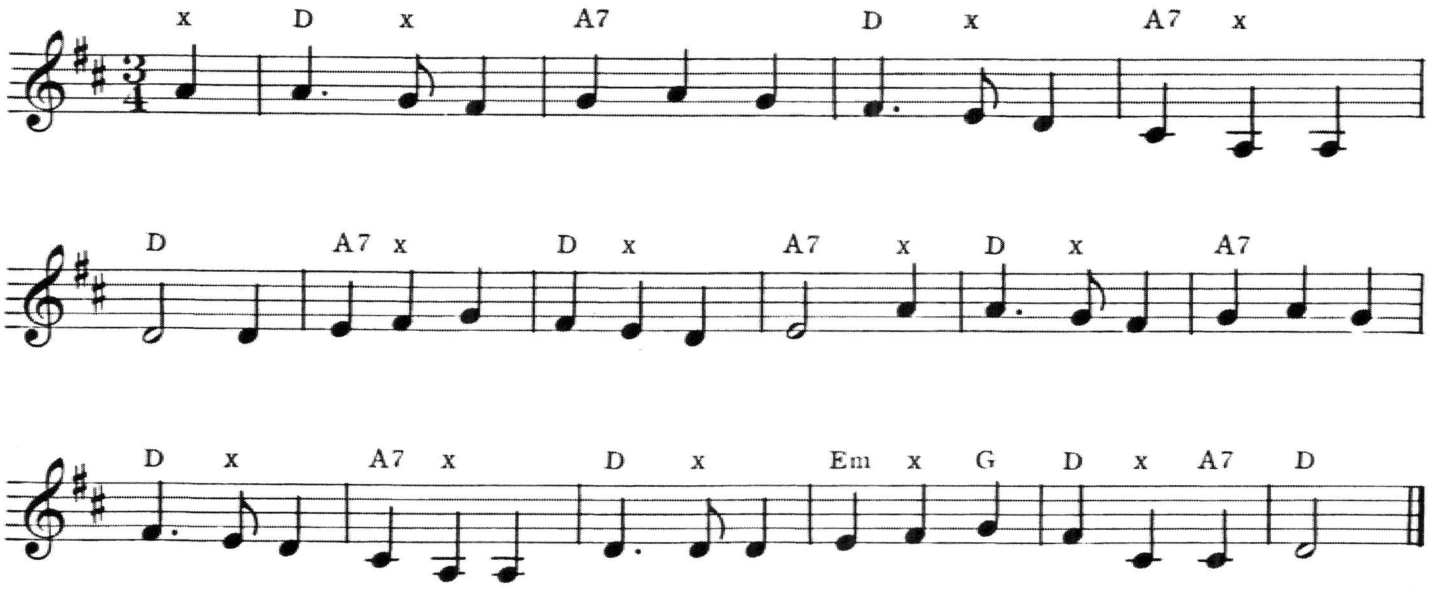


## AROUND HER HAIR SHE WORE A YELLOW RIBBON

# HARMONIZING THE NON-CHORDAL TONES WITH THE D CHORD

THE CHORDAL TONES | THE NON-CHORDAL TONES

THE NON-CHORDAL TONES HARMONIZED WITH THE D CHORD

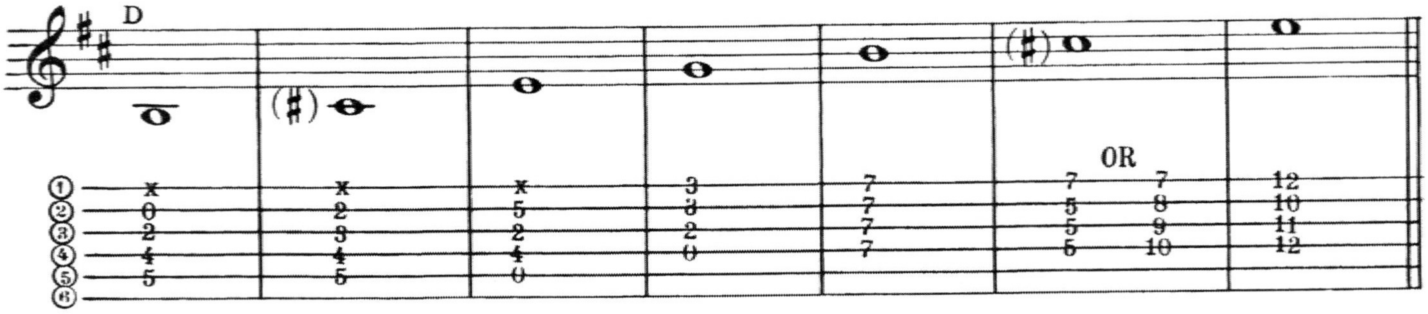


See page 20 for harmonizing the non-chordal tones with the G chord.
See page 30 for harmonizing the non-chordal tones with the A7 chord.

A NON-CHORDAL STUDY IN D

THE MAJOR CHORDS

The three principal chords in each major or minor key are the tonic, sub-dominant and the dominant seventh. They are so named because they are built on the scale tones so named. (See page 24).

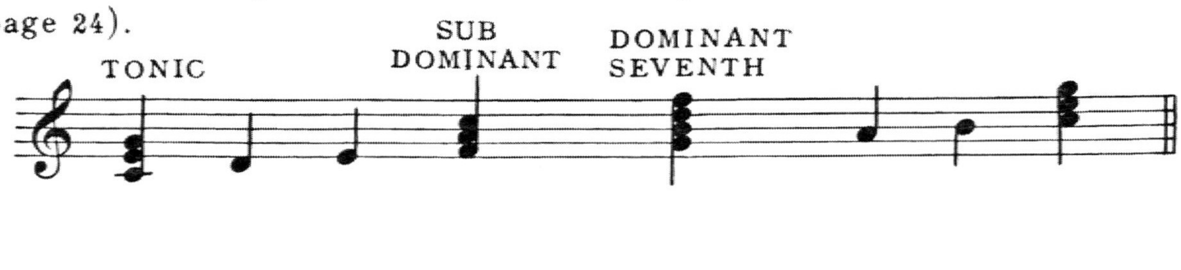

# THE MELODY CHORDS IN THE KEY OF B MINOR

(RELATIVE TO D MAJOR)

The chords in the key of B minor are Bm, Em and F#7

**CHORD SPELLING: B-D-F#** THE Bm CHORDS

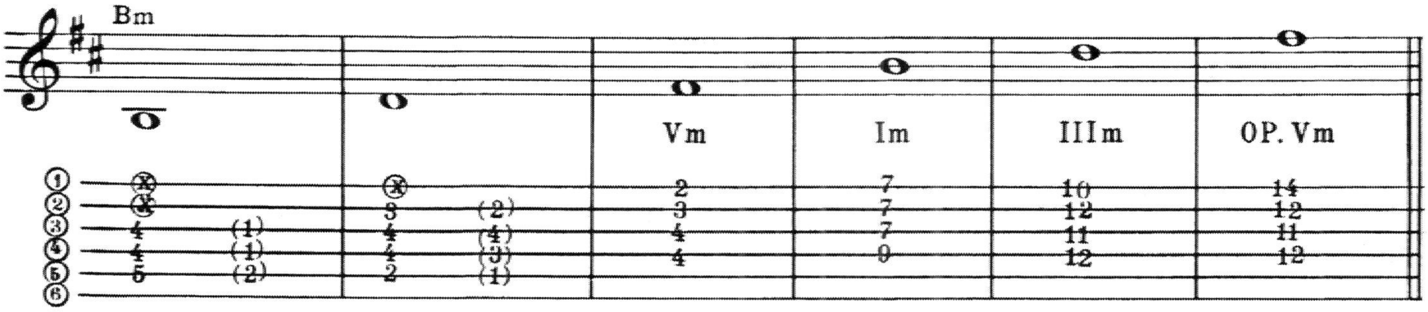


**CHORD SPELLING: E-G-B** THE Em CHORDS

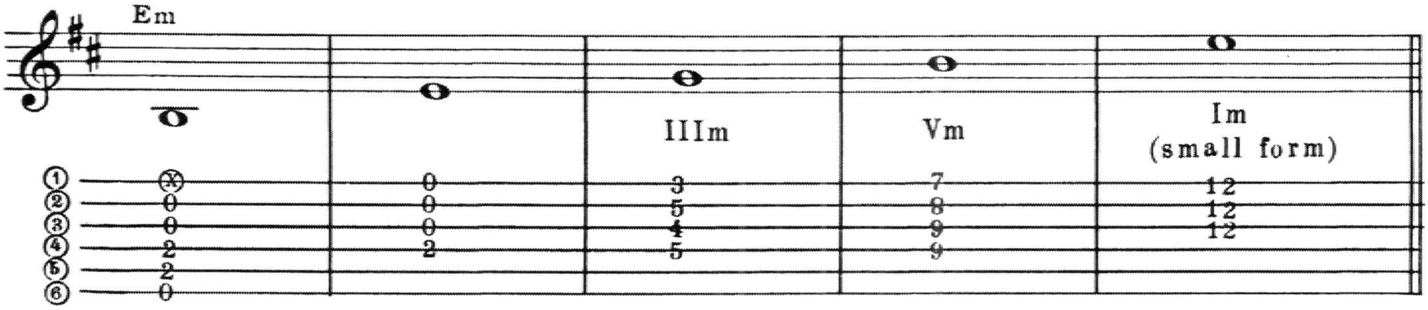


**CHORD SPELLING: F#-A#-C#-E** THE F#7 CHORDS

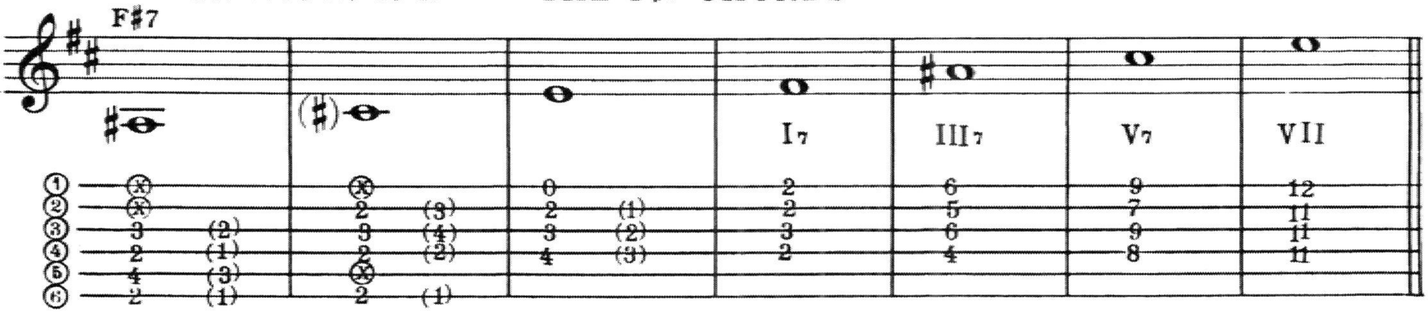


## CHORD STUDY IN B MINOR

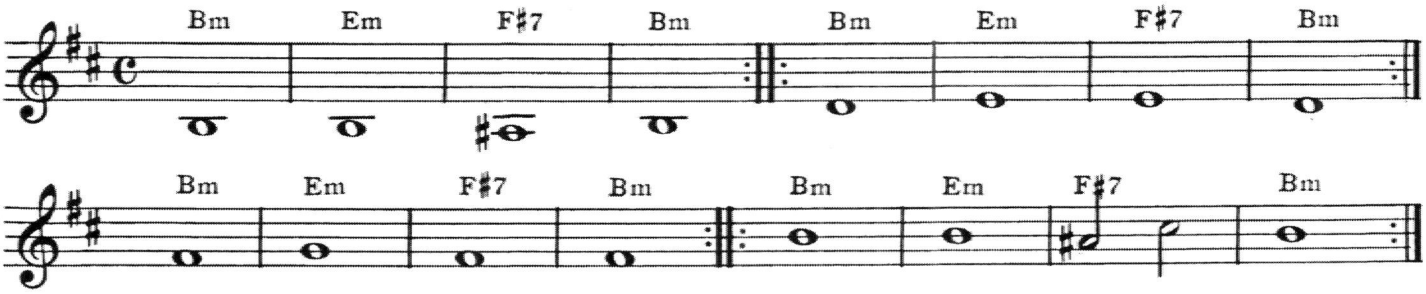


## THE HARMONIZED SCALE

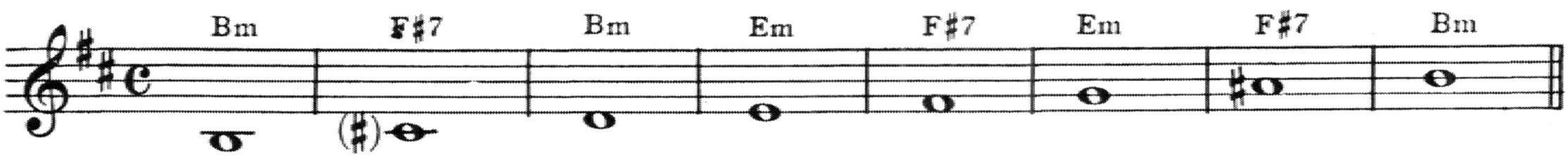


Practice ascending and descending.

## HARMONIZING THE NON-CHORDAL TONES WITH THE Bm CHORD

THE CHORDAL TONES

THE NON-CHORDAL TONES

THE NON-CHORDAL TONES HARMONIZED WITH THE Bm CHORD

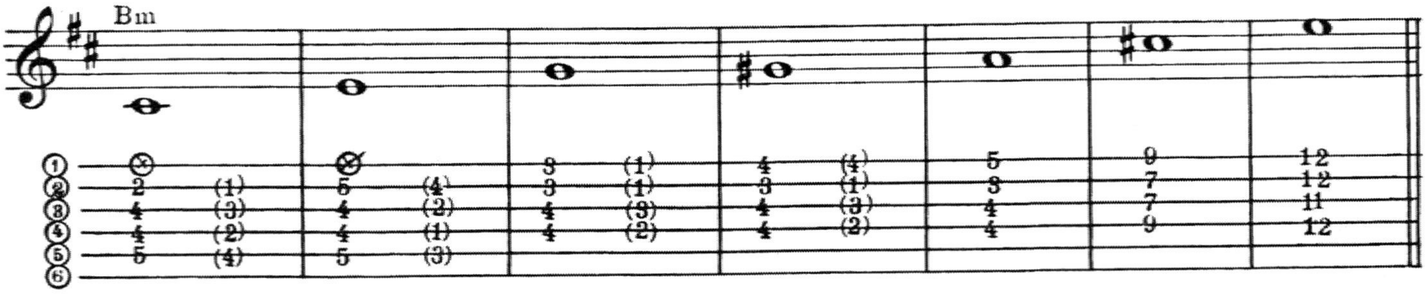


See page 24 for harmonizing the non-chordal tones with the Em chord.

## HARMONIZING THE NON-CHORDAL TONES WITH THE F♯7 CHORD

THE CHORDAL TONES

THE NON-CHORDAL TONES

THE NON-CHORDAL TONES HARMONIZED WITH THE F♯7 CHORD

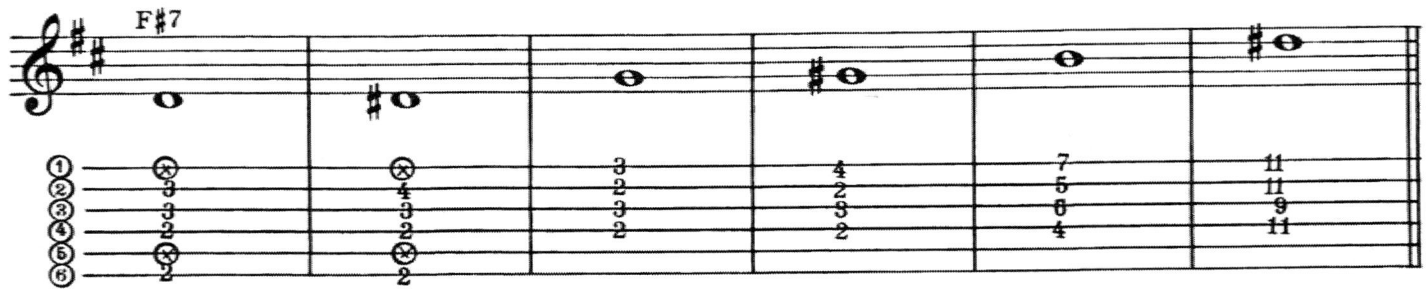


## CHANSON TRISTE

Slow

Tschaikowsky

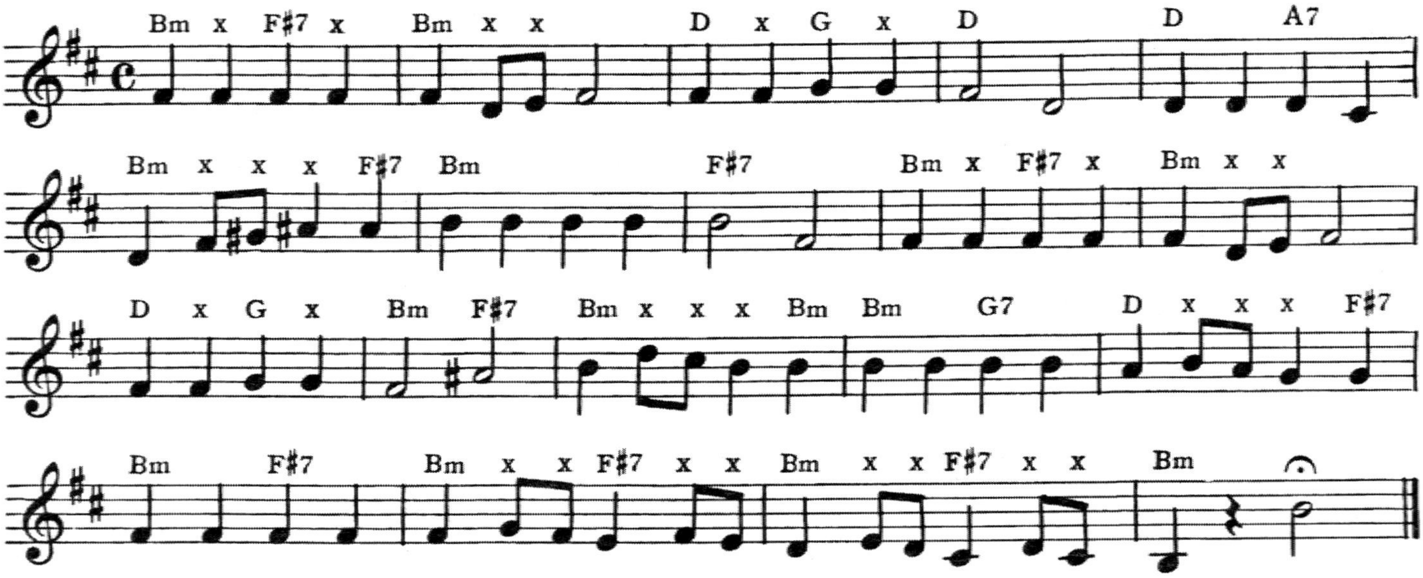